SPY CLASSRO

Sara's Meadow of Opportunity

code name
MEADOW

code name
FLOWER GARDEN

code name
PANDEMONIUM

A Girl Growing Up

SPY CLASSROOM 08

Sara's Meadow of Opportunity

Takemachi
ILLUSTRATION BY Tomari

New York

SPY CLASSROOM 08

Translation by Nathaniel Thrasher
Cover art by Tomari
Assistance with firearm research: Asaura

Yen On
150 West 30th Street
New York, NY 10001

Visit us at yenpress.com
facebook.com/yenpress
twitter.com/yenpress
yenpress.tumblr.com
instagram.com/yenpress

First Yen On Edition: September 2024
Edited by Yen On Editorial: Anna Powers
Designed by Yen Press Design: Andy Swist

Yen On is an imprint of Yen Press, LLC.
The Yen On name and logo are trademarks of Yen Press, LLC.

Library of Congress Cataloging-in-Publication Data
Names: Takemachi, author. | Tomari, Meron, illustrator. | Thrasher, Nathaniel Hiroshi, translator.
Title: Spy classroom / Takemachi ; illustrated by Tomari ; translation by Nathaniel Thrasher.
Other titles: Spy kyoushitsu. English
Description: First Yen On edition. | New York, NY : Yen On, 2021.
Identifiers: LCCN 2021021119 | ISBN 9781975322403 (v. 1 ; trade paperback) | ISBN 9781975322427 (v. 2 ; trade paperback)
Subjects: | CYAC: Spies—Fiction. | Schools—Fiction.
Classification: LCC PZ7.1.T343 Sp 2021 | DDC [Fic]—dc23
LC record available at https://lccn.loc.gov/2021021119

ISBNs: 978-1-9753-6751-0 (paperback)
978-1-9753-6752-7 (ebook)

10 9 8 7 6 5 4 3 2 1

LSC-C

Printed in the United States of America

CONTENTS

SPY CLASSROOM
Specialized lessons for an impossible mission
Code name: Meadow

CHARACTER PROFILES

Bonfire

Klaus

Lamplight's founder and the Greatest Spy in the World.

Flower Garden

Lily

A naive girl from the backcountry.

Daughter Dearest

Grete

A quiet girl and the daughter of a major politician.

Pandemonium

Sybilla

A brave girl and the daughter of a gangster.

Glint

Monika

An arrogant girl born into a family of artists.

Dreamspeaker

Thea

An elegant girl and the only child of a major newspaper company's president.

Meadow

Sara

A timid girl whose parents run a small restaurant.

Forgetter

Annette

A simple girl with no memories. Her origins are unknown.

Fool

Erna

An unlucky girl who frequently gets into accidents. Also, a former aristocrat.

Team Avian

Flock

Vindo

Glide

Qulle

South Wind

Queneau

Cloud Drift

Lan

Lander

Vics

Feather

Pharma

The CIM from the Fend Commonwealth

Hide—CIM Leadership

Cursemaster
Nathan

Magician
Mirena

Three Others

Belias—Hide's Personal Counterintelligence Unit

Puppeteer
Amelie

Lotus Doll, Disintegrator Doll, etc.

Vanajin—CIM's Largest Counterintelligence Unit

Armorer
Meredith

Swordsmith
Miné

Other

Silhouette
Luke

Tracker
Sylvette

Jester
Heine

Tunekeeper
Khaki

Team Inferno

Hearth	Firewalker	Soot
Veronika	**Gerde**	**Lukas**
Scapulimancer	Flamefanner	Torchlight
Wille	**Heide**	**Guido**

Team Serpent from the Galgad Empire

	White Spider	Blue Fly
	Silver Cicada	Purple Ant
Green Butterfly	Indigo Grasshopper	Black Mantis

Prologue

Machinations

To Sara, Monika was like a second teacher.

"All right, Sara. One more round."

"Okay. I'm ready."

Her main teacher, Klaus, was no good when it came to giving specific instructions. He wasn't particularly eloquent, and all his advice ended up being uselessly abstract. However, Monika was different.

"You need to be more decisive!"

Even smack-dab in the middle of their sparring match, she continued giving Sara specific, pointed advice.

"When someone spots you and you're too close to use your gun, you need to call in your hawk ASAP! Doesn't matter how hard you try; you're never gonna beat me solo!"

Monika bore down on Sara with her blunted knife, pummeling her with blows too fast for Sara to keep up with. Sara did her best to defend herself, but little by little, she was getting pushed back.

"But that said, you gotta stop running the same gambit over and over! You should be hiding your pigeon and mice in your hat and clothes so you can catch your opponent by surprise. Using your dog's nose to sniff out their lies. Don't just go for the obvious moves."

Monika let up with her knife just long enough to grab Sara by the shirt. Before Sara even had a chance to gasp in surprise, Monika had already swept her legs out from under her and hurled her through the air.

Sara landed ignobly on her backside, and Monika shot a stern look down at her. "You need to get your act together. The way you are now, you can't even protect yourself."

"U-understood..."

The two of them were practicing in the Heat Haze Palace courtyard. Monika was handling Sara's training while Klaus was out on a mission. She never minced words, but her advice was always on point.

Sara had been working under Monika's tutelage for a bit over four months. Monika drilled her on everything from negotiation tactics to infiltration techniques, but the bulk of her lessons were centered on self-defense. That largely translated to getting beaten up by Monika over and over. Sara always ended their sparring sessions too drained to even stand up.

That day was no exception, and once again, she was lying sprawled out on the courtyard ground. She was starting to get sick of this view of the clear blue sky.

Like always, she was bone-tired, but it was a satisfying kind of tired.

"But I am getting stronger, right?" After catching her breath, she smiled and looked up at Monika. "I can feel myself building up muscle. Maybe now I'm strong enough to handle some of the fighting my—"

"Just don't."

"What?"

The look in Monika's eyes as she stood over Sara was as cold as ice. "Remember what I told you in Longchon? It's not your job to fight. I'm just teaching you so you can keep yourself safe. Don't go trying to show off."

"But..."

There was something almost refreshing about how harsh Monika was being.

"That's not what you should be shooting for," her tutor continued coolly as she took a swig from her water bottle.

All Sara could do was clutch her head and groan. Monika was 100 percent right. No matter how hard Sara worked, she would never be able to become like Sybilla or Monika, who could eliminate their foes and steal information with nothing but their raw combat prowess. She just wasn't built that way.

However, there was a part of her that didn't want to accept that.
"Then what should my goal be?"
"That's something you have to decide for yourself."
Monika plopped down on the ground next to Sara.

"You have to be the one to figure it out. What sort of ideals do you have as a spy? How do you want to fight? What kind of life do you want to live?"

That was an impossibly difficult question to answer.
For starters, Sara didn't have any proactive reason for wanting to be a spy. She merely ended up at a spy academy so she could cover her room and board after her parents lost their jobs. She didn't *have* any ideals.
"Don't worry," she heard Monika say as she puzzled over the question in silence. "I'll stick with you till you find your answer."
Monika didn't meet her gaze. Sara thought she saw her cheeks turn a bit red, but she wasn't sure if she was imagining things or not.
As hopeless a pupil as Sara was, Monika never abandoned her.
Even during the period that Lamplight spent in close contact with Avian—their so-called honeymoon—Sara continued training under Monika. One of Avian's members, "Glide" Qulle, tried to get in on the teaching-Sara action, but with a brusque "*Buzz off*," Monika sent her packing. In the end, Sara only ended up taking a single lesson from Qulle.
"All right, time for another round."
Monika thumped Sara on the shoulder and urged her back to her feet. The look in Monika's eyes was one of exasperation, but there was a kindness shining through it, and that was what Sara adored about her.

The world was awash in pain.
In order to unravel the reason why their Avian comrades were killed, the Din Republic spy team Lamplight went undercover in the Fend Commonwealth. After facing off against the Commonwealth's

CIM intelligence agency, Lamplight ultimately discovered that their nemesis Serpent had been the ones pulling the strings.

Serpent's plan had been to assassinate Prince Darryn, a member of the Fend royal family, and to pin the blame for the crime on a Din spy. What's more, they took advantage of that fact to extort Lamplight member "Glint" Monika into turning traitor. By forcing Monika to run a covert op for them, their hope was that they would be able to exhaust Lamplight's boss, "Bonfire" Klaus.

However, Monika double-crossed them and made some moves of her own. By willingly taking the blame for Prince Darryn's assassination, she was able to resolve the entire situation.

That said, the price it cost her was steep. After a fierce battle against the CIM's spies, she was forced to beat a retreat and ended up getting attacked by Serpent. White Spider and Black Mantis had her surrounded.

In her last few moments, she used her radio to pass intel on Serpent along to Lamplight…

"I'm in love with you."

…and after she professed her love to Lily, the call cut out.

"I'm going to defeat White Spider!!"

Sara's eyes were teary as she made her declaration.

Three days after Lamplight lost contact with Monika, the CIM counterintelligence team Belias came to see them. They needed to keep Lamplight under surveillance, so they announced that they would be taking Klaus and Thea into custody.

Monika's betrayal had cost Lamplight dearly.

Not only was Klaus under suspicion for having been her boss, but Thea was arrested as well for having assisted Monika by forming the anti-establishment Fires of War organization. Meanwhile, Grete had been left severely weakened after Monika kidnapped and imprisoned her, Annette suffered a series of broken ribs when Monika attacked her, and Erna had gotten badly hurt taking a CIM bullet in order to save Monika from a dire predicament. The three of them were all recovering in the hospital. And as for Monika herself, it wasn't even clear if she was alive or not.

With Lamplight functionally out of commission, it was Sara who rose to the occasion. She called out to Klaus right before he got transferred from their previous cell to a new location.

She knew full well how unrealistic it was to think that she might defeat White Spider. White Spider was a member of the mysterious Galgad intelligence unit Serpent, and he was the man who'd assassinated the Commonwealth's crown prince and plunged the nation into turmoil. The thought of Sara being able to apprehend him was downright absurd.

However, White Spider was the only one who knew where Monika was.

When he heard Sara's pledge, Klaus didn't laugh. He just narrowed his eyes a little.

"Magnificent." His voice was calm. "I'll leave it to you, then. I know you're up to the task."

That was the last thing he said before Belias hauled him off.

With the room suddenly much emptier, Sara let out a long breath. The adrenaline from her bold declaration caused her heart to pound in her chest. She had no intention of taking back what she'd said, of course, but still.

As she felt her pulse quicken, she heard a pair of voices from either side of her.

"And what the hell you think you're doin', tryin' to hog all the glory?"

"Yeah, what she said. Did you forget about your super-duper reliable friends here or something?"

The two friends in question grinned as they each slung an arm over one of Sara's shoulders.

Sara couldn't help but smile as well. "Miss Sybilla, Miss Lily."

"Pandemonium" Sybilla was a white-haired girl with courage in her eyes and a toned physique, and "Flower Garden" Lily was a silver-haired girl notable for her adorably childish face and sizable bust.

"Of course I haven't forgotten you," Sara told them. And it was the honest truth. She'd simply gotten a little carried away, that was all. "Let's get him, the three of us. There's no way I could do this alone."

The duo gave her hearty replies—"Hell yeah," and "You don't have to tell me twice"—and thumped her on the back.

Sybilla flashed the group an awkwardly toothy smile. "Y'know, it really brings me back, havin' the three of us team up like this. We haven't done this since, what, the Corpse mission?"

"Yeah, I remember that," Lily agreed. "That time when the three of us disguised ourselves as maids."

Sara nodded. "That's right. Back then, we were the ones who got left out of the actual mission."

"Though if ya think about it, Grete was the one the boss gave the most responsibility to outta everyone," Sybilla noted. "End of the day, the only ones who *really* got left outta the Corpse mission were us three."

"Grrr. How dare he leave the one and only Lily out on the sidelines! Even now, I still haven't forgiven him for that!"

"Ha-ha-ha. You really know how to hold a grudge, Miss Lily."

"Lookin' back now, he made the right call. Back then, Monika, Grete, and Thea were savin' our asses left and right."

"I can't really deny that," Lily replied. "But this time..."

"...it's our turn to be the heroes," Sara said.

Now that they'd talked it over, Sybilla thrust her fist high in the air. "Let's fuckin' do this, Unchosen Squad!"

"You can say that again!" "We got this!"

The whole conversation had been far peppier than befitted a group of spies. It was a testament to their immaturity, but also to their readiness to hold strong before any adversity.

Diego Kruger was a novelist with a cocaine problem.

Diego had gotten his start writing historical novels, but when the public started going gaga over mystery fiction, his publisher ordered him to pivot. In Diego's eyes, though, historical literature was the finest genre there was, and mysteries were for philistines. Every time he wrote one, he found it harder to breathe. His stomach did backflips.

He tore out his hair. Occasionally, he even turned to drink to forcibly drown his sorrows.

Before he knew it, alcohol wasn't doing it for him anymore. He needed something stronger, and that was how he got involved with drugs. His wife had long since left him, but he chose not to think about that. He needed to finish a manuscript, any manuscript, and so he drifted into a syringe-fueled reverie in his suburban apartment.

It was that very same apartment that the Galgad spy team Serpent was using as a hideout.

One of Serpent's members—White Spider—sat on the sofa smoking a cigarette and counting a stack of bills. His head looked like a giant mushroom, his eyes were dull and gloomy, and his skin was worryingly pallid. Due to his atrocious posture, he looked a fair bit shorter than he actually was. Even his own allies mocked him for looking "creepy" and "like a loser."

He repeatedly clicked his tongue in irritation as he turned the bills over with his skinny fingers.

A voice came from behind his back.

"Are you sure the junkie writer didn't bite it?"

The speaker's dark hood made it impossible to see his face, but White Spider could tell from the height and the three right arms extending from his coat that the man was an ally. The two extra arms gleamed with a mechanical light as they lay coiled around his brawny real arm with its countless scars.

His name was Black Mantis, and he too was a member of Serpent.

White Spider shot a glance over at Diego's prone form over in the corner of the room. "Naaah, he just had a bad trip and pissed himself again. Clean it up, would ya?"

"Why should I have to do that?"

"'Cause I'm working, can't you see that? Turns out the old bastard doesn't have as much of a nest egg as I thought he would. Shit, man, I thought writers made money hand over fist."

White Spider ran his fingers through his hair as he glared at the bankbook he'd stolen from Diego. He'd been hoping for a capital injection from the homeland, but he couldn't get in touch with their smuggler. They must have gotten picked up by the CIM. In the end, White Spider had been reduced to getting some idiot novelist hooked on drugs and pumping him for money.

"Then I suppose that settles it." Black Mantis heaved a sigh and sat down on the sofa across from White Spider. "We can't continue the mission. I'm retiring."

White Spider hunched over even more and buried his face in his hands. "You can't just announce your retirement like you're commenting on the weather."

Not only was White Spider single-handedly responsible for all of Serpent's coordination, budgeting, and weapons procurement, he was also in charge of keeping the rest of the team appeased. Considering how full of eccentrics their roster was, that was a full-time job and then some.

"I dunno how you can be taking things this well," White Spider continued. "Thanks to that damn Glint kid, my whole plan just went to hell in a—"

"Then we should just go home," Black Mantis said. "We've completed our mission. Our job was to kill Prince Darryn and Mia Godolphin. I am a little worried about Firewalker's investigation notes, but not enough to overextend myself for them."

"...Yeah, maybe you have a point."

"Is it really that important that we kill Bonfire?"

Upon hearing his nemesis's name, White Spider stopped midway through turning over a bill.

"Half of it is just spite," he replied. "He's the one who killed Silver Cicada and got Purple Ant thrown in the slammer."

"You're so petty."

"Oh, shut up. You know the other half just as well as I do."

White Spider spat his cigarette onto the floor and crushed it underfoot.

"Before long, he's going to pick up where Hearth left off and commit *the evilest crime in human history.*"

He shot Black Mantis a harsh glare.

"Watching him beat Purple Ant made me positive of that. I should've seen it earlier. Eventually, he's gonna find out the truth about Hearth, and when that happens, there'll be no stopping him. He'll be the scariest enemy Serpent has ever seen. I'm sure of it."

"You really think the situation is that serious?"

"We gotta do this, whatever it takes. I mean it when I say we're standing at a turning point in history. If we fuck this up, the weak won't stand a chance in this world anymore." White Spider reached over and picked up his trusty sniper rifle. "If there's one spy we've absolutely gotta kill, it's him. And right now is a huge opportunity. He's got a wounded leg, and the CIM's got him locked up."

White Spider had the inside scoop. The original plan had been to have Green Butterfly use Monika to run Klaus even further into the ground, but even though she'd failed to do so, she'd still dealt him a considerable wound. If Serpent wanted to choke the life out of him, this was the best chance they were going to get.

Black Mantis raised his right arm as though to show off his prosthetics. "Like I told you before, I'm not at my strongest. My Surmounters are damaged." The Surmounters were what he called his two fake arms. He could control them as he pleased, and between their burning, cleaving, and smashing capabilities, they allowed him to easily perform feats that would have been far beyond most people. "Repairing them in full would require a trip back to Galgad. I've put in some stopgap repairs, but it's only a temporary solution."

"Yeah, I know."

"Still, I'll do what I can. I may be in poor form, but I remain the Unrivaled. A hero never turns down those in need."

"That's good to hear."

"What should we do about Green Butterfly? She's been captured. Should we save her?"

"She'll figure something out on her own. She's a part of Serpent, too, after all."

"Very well. By the way, I'm going to cut your hair. Hold still."

Without waiting for a response, Black Mantis put his prosthetics into motion. They extended out as if the seven feet between him and White Spider was nothing, whizzing past White Spider's face and scattering a shower of hair in their wake.

A huge mass fell into White Spider's lap.

"..Huh?"

"It was drawing too much attention. I'll be going now."

With that short goodbye, Black Mantis left the room without so much as looking back.

White Spider couldn't muster the energy to come up with a witty quip. A weak "My hair..." was all he could muster, but there was no one around to hear him.

With the foul smell of human discharge wafting through the air, White Spider let out a sigh.

He'd finished counting the bills by that point, and after shoving them in his pocket, he took out a pair of scissors and a hand mirror and tried to at least make his hair look presentable.

As the scissors glided across his head, he felt his thoughts sharpen in turn.

This is fine. The question is, how do I proceed?

He didn't have any time to waste; he continued honing his plan to kill Klaus.

The biggest thing weighing on his mind was that final message Monika had left to her team.

"Get code name Insight. We need them. They're the only person who can beat Serpent."

He needed to figure it out.

Who's Insight?

No obvious candidates sprang to mind, and White Spider had data on every spy in the Din Republic. Guido had given Serpent the keys to the kingdom when he betrayed Inferno. "Bonfire" Klaus didn't have any allies he was especially close to aside from Inferno, and aside from Bonfire himself, all of Inferno had been wiped out. There wasn't a single power player in Din who hadn't gotten their intel leaked.

Given all that information, who exactly was it that had the power to beat Serpent? Was there really someone Klaus was willing to put that faith in? No, there was no way.

Was it a bluff, then? But to what end?

Did White Spider actually need to come up with a countermeasure?

Or was he overthinking things, and this was just a ploy to throw him off-balance?

"Eh, at least they're keeping things interesting. Me, I'm ready to end this once and for all. If they wanna fight to the bitter end, then more power to 'em."

White Spider finished working with the scissors and combed back his hair.

"Let's do this, you monster. Serpent and Lamplight. One last game of cat and mouse."

The spy known as code name Insight quietly observed the Fend Commonwealth capital Hurough from atop a building's roof.

In the back of their head, they thought back to their conversation with Klaus.

One chilly evening, Klaus came and visited Insight when they were in bed. It wasn't the first time they'd met, but Klaus's face was tense all the same.

"I'm going to be honest here. I need to ask for your help."

Klaus bowed low.

Insight was surprised by the gesture. Klaus's behavior usually carried hints of arrogance in it, and it was unlike him to humble himself so.

"Lamplight has fought Serpent a number of times now, and they've probably gotten ahold of a fair bit of intel on us. If we want to catch them off-guard, we need a new tool in our repertoire," Klaus said. "I want you to become Lamplight's newest spy."

"........."

Insight had no idea how to respond to that.

They returned Klaus's gaze in silence, to which Klaus responded with a nod. "With your leave, I'd like to give you a new code name—Insight. That's what we'll call you."

With another deep bow, Klaus asked Insight to look out for the team. It was a side of him the girls never got to see.

After seeing Klaus show his conviction in his own sort of way, Insight gave him a slight nod.

As they finished reminiscing on their exchange with Klaus, Insight exhaled.

The time for them to make their move was fast approaching. The only problem was finding the right opening. The thing was, they themselves were Lamplight's strategy. They absolutely couldn't afford to have their identity exposed.

It was their responsibility as Lamplight's newest member to save the entire team. Failure wasn't an option.

Chapter 1
Rearing

Klaus grimaced at his restraints. They'd been constructed with cutting-edge CIM technology, and they were impressively sturdy. Not only was he being confined in a detention room, but he could also barely move his arms.

Klaus wasn't pleased about the situation, but even he had to admit that it was the right call for the CIM to make. They wanted his help capturing the Serpent members who'd been involved in the royal assassination, but they couldn't afford to give him any sort of unilateral trust, especially not after "Flash Fire" Monika had just come straight out of his inner circle.

He could help, but only on a short leash.

It was hardly the most equal set of terms, but Klaus had no choice but to accept them. Several of Lamplight's members were recuperating at a CIM-controlled hospital, making them hostages in everything but name.

Klaus wasn't allowed to leave his room. It was locked from the outside, and they'd confiscated all his weapons. He had a bed and a toilet, and they fed him and sent a doctor to check up on him, but he didn't have access to a newspaper. Unsurprisingly, they also prevented him from having any contact with his team.

In short, he was cut off from being able to do just about any spy work.

"My, how the tables have turned."

When Amelie visited the room, her voice was dripping with sarcasm.

Amelie—that was to say, "Puppeteer" Amelie—was in charge of Belias, the counterintelligence team that answered directly to the CIM's senior leadership and had been facing off against Lamplight as of late. She was a woman in her late twenties with a Gothic outfit and heavy bags under her eyes. The frills adorning her dress were in stark contrast with the grim air she carried herself with.

"Now it's *your* turn to behave yourself under *my* supervision."

"What, are you still holding a grudge?" Up until just a few days prior, Klaus had been holding Amelie's agents hostage and forcing her to obey his orders. "This is no time to be acting childish. We both need to let bygones be bygones."

"How awfully convenient for you."

"It's for your own good. I haven't forgiven you people, and I'd be perfectly happy going right back at your throats." Klaus took a seat on the chair beside him. "The only reasons I'm going along with this are out of respect for Monika's wishes and because I think you can be useful."

"Heh. Bold words for a man with a mangled leg."

With a thin, mocking smile, Amelie cast her gaze down to Klaus's left thigh. That was where he'd been shot during his duel with Monika. Due to how much he'd been using it since then, his wound had gotten even worse.

Thanks to Amelie's keen powers of observation, she could tell just how far Klaus was from being able to fight in peak form.

"Rest assured we have no problems making ourselves useful as long as you return the favor." She sat down on the chair across from his. "Tomorrow evening, a representative from Hide is coming to see you."

"In person?"

Hide, the CIM's senior leadership, was a group shrouded in mystery. They were Amelie's direct superiors. Klaus had been trying to make contact with them for ages, and it looked like he was finally getting his wish.

"These are extraordinary circumstances. Even I've only seen his face once before. Together, we're going to hold a strategy meeting on how we intend to capture White Spider." After Klaus nodded in assent, Amelie shot him a biting look. "Before that, though, there's something I need to know."

"What's that?"

"Meadow's statement just now. Was that made in earnest?"

She was doubtless referring to when Sara had said she would defeat White Spider. It was a daring claim, and it had been highly out of character for Sara to make it.

"I imagine so," Klaus replied without a moment's hesitation. "I don't doubt her conviction. She wants to save Monika. The two of them were mentor and mentee, and to be honest, it was such an effective setup it gave me concerns for my job security."

"I see."

"That said, I can't deny that I'm worried about her ability to pull it off."

It sounded harsh, but Sara was still working on hitting her stride. Klaus had the utmost confidence in her talents, but at present, it was hard to draw favorable comparisons between her and the others.

What's more, there was another major concern weighing on his mind.

"There's something eerie about White Spider."

"Eerie? That's a rather abstract way of putting it…"

"From what I've seen of him, the man is a loser through and through. There's no dignity to anything he says or does, and as much as he likes to wail about how he's going to kill me, he doesn't hesitate to flee as fast as his legs will carry him the minute it looks like things are going south for him."

Klaus had encountered White Spider on three occasions.

The first was in the Galgad Empire, when White Spider killed Guido. The second was in the Din Republic, right in the middle of the incident with Annette's mother. And the third was in the United States of Mouzaia, right after Klaus finished apprehending Purple Ant.

By all accounts, the man was highly skilled—yet for some reason, the impression of him as a loser was impossible to shake.

"The things Serpent's been doing here in Fend… They don't track with what I know about him."

"Could you be more specific?"

"If I described it as being like a glass of water with a single gram of paint in it, would that help explain it?"

"I assure you it would not."

"Well, that's fine. The point is, Sara said that she was prepared to do it. I'm going to choose to believe in her."

Klaus would be lying if he said he wasn't worried, but he'd chosen to take a gamble on them, and he intended to let that gamble ride. The girls had grown in ways he never would have imagined. Not even his famed intuition could have prepared him for how suddenly and how radically they would improve.

There was a certain delicacy to the way Amelie lowered her tone. "Are you certain about this?"

"Hmm?"

"I respect your position, I sincerely do. But if those young ladies want to apprehend White Spider, they're going to run into a serious obstacle."

There were hints of embarrassment flitting in and out of her expression. It was unlike her.

Klaus asked her to explain herself.

"I believe it goes without saying that we aren't going to arrest those three. I imagine you would object if we did."

"Of course. That's a basic prerequisite for my cooperation."

"And rightly so. However, we can't exactly allow them to roam about freely, either."

"........."

"Aside from Belias and Hide, the rest of the CIM's operatives believe that 'Flash Fire' Monika was the one who assassinated Prince Darryn. And they know that she used to belong to Lamplight."

Klaus wasn't happy about it, but that was what Monika wanted, so that was the way things were. By passing herself off as a Serpent member and taking the heat for everything, she'd prevented the situation from getting even more out of hand.

By the sound of it, though, her doing so had given rise to some new problems.

"As a result," Amelie said apologetically, "most of the CIM holds Lamplight in extreme contempt."

After tasting freedom for the first time in three days, the girls found themselves staring down an unexpected roadblock.

When the room they were confined in got unlocked at around one in the afternoon, they immediately rushed out. Their first order of business was to track down White Spider's whereabouts. They'd already decided what their initial move was going to be, and time was of the essence. Every second mattered. The three of them marched confidently down the hallway.

When they got to the entrance, though, they were greeted by a shrill female voice.

"Ah-ha-ha, you punks really thought we'd just let you waltz on out of here?!"

A woman dressed in a suit charged at them from around the corner. She was clutching a spherical device in her hand, and she held it up as though showing it off.

"Absolute Reverb."

""""——!!""""

The girls reflexively braced themselves, but their defenses were useless against the attack. A thunderous peal blared out from the sphere. It felt like their ears were going to split open, and the noise traveled right through their heads and rattled their brains. If they'd taken even a second longer to clamp their hands over their ears, their eardrums might well have burst.

None of them were able to stay upright, not after taking an attack like that. All they could do was crouch on the floor and try to endure until the noise went away.

"We invented this little baby to use against terrorists," the woman boasted once she stopped her audio onslaught. "Stings, doesn't it? Ha-ha!"

Sara stared back at her in blank shock.

Wh-what is this woman's problem?!

Using a sonic weapon on someone the moment you met them was an act of absolute lunacy.

The woman's hair was buzzed almost down to the skin. You rarely ever saw haircuts that short, even in the city. For her outfit, she was wearing a double-breasted suit adorned with a collection of badges. She appeared to be in her late twenties.

She gave the girls a contemptuous look as she introduced herself.

"Say hello to one of Vanajin's aides-de-camp, 'Swordsmith' Miné! I'm only gonna say that once, so make sure you remember it, handmaids!"

Her tone was chipper, but there was something oddly combative about it.

Sara and Lily couldn't help but exchange a glance and a surly "Oh, you're with *them*..."

Vanajin was the CIM's largest counterintelligence unit, and Lamplight didn't like them one bit. They were the ones who'd locked the girls in there in the first place. They were also the ones who'd taken Sara and Lan hostage.

Undeterred by the girls' naked animosity, Miné continued on. "I'm here to keep an eye on you punks. I'll be with you twenty-four seven, and don't you forget it!"

"Keep an eye on us? What are you talking about?"

"Ah-ha-ha, we're not just gonna let a bunch of Flash Fire's old teammates wander around free! Do you handmaids seriously not get that?!"

Sara immediately picked up on what was happening.

The vast majority of the CIM's spies were unaware of the truth about Monika. There was no way they were just going to let the Lamplight girls run free.

"What the hell are you comin' at us for?" Sybilla said, rising to her feet and getting up in Miné's face. "The way I heard it, we're supposed to be helpin' each other. The whole idea was that Lamplight and the CIM would work together to take down White Spider—"

"Ah-ha-ha, sounds like someone let their ego run away with them," Miné replied, not backing down. "We need help from you people like we need a hole in the head."

With her smile unbroken, she held up her spherical weapon.

Once again, that same thunderous roar blasted out. The sonic assault made the girls feel like their heads were going to explode.

"You're just Bonfire's little handmaids. We know better than to expect you to accomplish anything," Miné mocked them after shutting off the sound waves.

Drool dribbled from Sara's mouth. There was nothing she could do but groan unintelligibly. Beside her, Sybilla and Lily were suffering the same.

That single attack had rendered them completely helpless. Despite their three-to-one advantage, Miné had completely overpowered them.

"The only reason for keeping you people alive is my orders from the top." Miné's voice cut through the ringing in their ears. "If you wanna try to shake me, be my guest. All of Vanajin will come together to end you. Ah-ha-ha. And just for the record, if you thought I was strong, my boss is a hundred times stronger."

Sybilla quietly clicked her tongue. "Tch..."

Through their gasps, Sara and Lily talked her down. "We need to back down for now, Miss Sybilla." "Yeah, we gotta just take it on the chin."

At the moment, getting into a fight with the CIM would be a bad move. The cards were stacked against them.

Lily put on her most amiable smile. "We read you loud and clear, Miné. I'm a big believer in doing what the strong say. I'm happy to go along with your terms. And if you need your boots licked, just say the word."

"Ah-ha-ha. Glad you know your place." Seeming quite pleased with that, Miné extended her foot Lily's way.

Lily pretended not to notice and went on. "As a matter of fact, there's actually somewhere I was hoping you could take us."

Humiliating as it was, they had little choice but to operate under the CIM's supervision for now. If they wanted to reach their first destination, they were going to need the CIM's help getting there.

On the state hospital grounds, there was an odd ward surrounded by multiple layers of fences.

The majority of the patients there were either CIM agents or spies those agents had captured, and the others were politicians and members of royalty whose ailments hadn't been made public. It was a ward designed for patients who, for whatever reason, couldn't use normal hospitals.

That was where Lily had asked Miné to take them. The CIM were the ones who managed the secret ward, and that was where a large number of Lamplight personnel and affiliates were being held.

When they got there, Miné gave them the rundown on the other girls' conditions.

"Cloud Drift is doing her rehab, so she's out on a monitored walk."

"Cloud Drift" Lan was the sole surviving member of Avian. She'd never received any proper treatment after getting attacked by Belias, but now she was on the mend.

"And you won't be able to see Forgetter. As a matter of fact, her room is completely off-limits."

"Huh?" Sybilla asked. "What's up with Annette?"

"She's awake, but she got agitated and started lashing out. They had to handcuff her to her bed like a wild animal, ha-ha."

When Monika betrayed them, she broke Annette's ribs and beat her half to death.

Annette's hospital room was visible from where they were, and Miné pointed out where it was. It was up on the fourth floor. There was a tiny open window, likely for ventilation reasons, and the sound of metal clanging against metal was audible from within.

Lily and Sybilla grimaced at their teammate's inhumane treatment.

Sara let out a quiet groan as well. "........." She'd brought her hawk along, and she stroked his head.

Miné grinned in amusement at their reactions, then continued her explanation. "Someone you *can* see is Fool. She's badly injured, though."

Sara and the others decided to head to her room—that was, Erna's room—first.

Miné led them there, and inside, they found Erna fast asleep.

In order to help Monika during her battle against the CIM, Erna had dived into a rain of bullets. By disguising herself as an ordinary civilian and intentionally letting herself get hit, she'd bought Monika time to take a breather. It was a distressing act of self-sacrifice...but if not for her, Monika likely would have died.

All else being equal, she would have come under heavy fire for having assisted Monika, but Amelie had pulled some strings and protected her.

"Leave the rest to us, 'kay?"

When Sybilla stroked her teammate's cheek, Erna let out a contented "Yeep..." in her sleep.

The girls decided to let her get her rest and left her some fruit as a get-well present before departing the room.

As they made their way to the final hospital room, Miné frowned. "Now, Daughter Dearest has been giving the nurses all sorts of headaches."

Sara, Lily, and Sybilla all cocked their heads in confusion. That was surprising to hear. Of all the girls on the team, Grete was rarely the one causing problems.

"Her body's practically breaking down, but she refuses to rest. And that's after she got held for over ten days with basically no food. Ah-ha-ha, the stupid girl can't even see how dire her situation is." Miné clicked her tongue in annoyance. "Can you lot talk some sense into her? I'm not happy about it, but I'm under strict orders to keep you all in good health."

When Miné told them that it would be faster for them to just see her for themselves, the girls quickened their pace toward Grete's room.

Lily threw open the door. "Is everything okay in here, Grete?"

"You're here!" Grete immediately spotted them from atop the bed, and her whole face lit up.

However, it was the trio coming into the room that was really in for a surprise. The entire area around the bed was packed to bursting with papers. Each and every sheet was completely full of fountain pen scribbles, and the bedside table had a newspaper, a map of Hurough, and a radio on it. By the look of it, Grete was copying down every bit of information she could get her hands on.

Lily rushed over to her teammate and gently scolded her. "Wh-what do you think you're doing? You need to get some rest!"

"This is more important. Right now, analysis is the only thing that I'm good for..."

Clearly, Grete was hard at work sorting through the mass of intel. Had she forced the nurses to bring her all that paper and all those pens?

"Th-that's actually a big help," Sara said, standing beside the bed as she broached the main topic. "To tell you the truth, Miss Grete, we actually came to get your advice."

That was the main reason they'd come to visit.

For all their talk about how they were going to capture White Spider, the girls had quickly gotten stuck. With how massive Hurough's population was, tracking down a single man was all but impossible. They didn't even have any leads.

In the end, the three of them had all come to the same conclusion.

"Bottom line is, I dunno what the hell we're supposed to do."

"...Just as I expected." Grete gave them a warm smile. "I've been collating information in order to pass it along to you."

"That's our tactician for ya," Sybilla said. "I always feel better knowin' you've got our back."

The three of them promptly gathered around the bed.

"Please, tell us how we can catch White Spider."

"I have two suggestions I'd like to put forth." Grete pointed at the map spread out on the bed. "The first is to go to Monika's last known location, the town of Immiran, and search the entire area."

Sara and the others nodded. That made perfect sense.

After her fierce fight against the CIM, Monika headed for a small town to the southeast of Hurough. That town was called Immiran, and that was where the hideout of an Inferno member named "Firewalker" Gerde was located. Monika had been heading there to use it as a safehouse.

A merry voice echoed out from a corner of the room. "Ah-ha-ha! My people already picked that area clean!" Miné laughed in amusement. "We found a burned-down building and what looked like the aftermath of a fight. But there was neither hide nor hair of Serpent anywhere around it! And we have no idea where that wretched Flash Fire is, either!"

Apparently, Klaus had already sent the CIM in to investigate. However, the heavy rain that started falling just after the whole thing went down had washed away any tracks or odors there may have been to find.

Grete seemed unperturbed by Miné's presence. "I see. If they failed to find a corpse, then there's a possibility that Serpent made off with Monika. Without any clues to follow up, though, it might be best to leave the search to the CIM."

It was a logical decision. Considering how unfamiliar they were with the area, searching around at random was unlikely to turn up much of anything.

"I believe we should bet on the following possibility."

When she went on, her voice rang with striking confidence.

"Around the time of Prince Darryn's funeral…we can capture White Spider *when he comes to kill the boss.*"

Sara blinked.

She was having trouble processing the suggestion. It felt like there were some logical leaps being made.

Sybilla was similarly bewildered, and she cocked her head in confusion. "Huh? What makes you think White Spider's gonna attack the boss?"

"As far as I can tell, White Spider has a peculiar obsession with him, and the boss is both injured and restrained. That presents an opportunity that White Spider wouldn't pass up, as far as I can tell. I believe the odds are quite good."

They thought back to what they'd heard the man say after their mission in Mitario.

"Next time, though, you're dead. You're getting to be a real pain in Serpent's butt. Seriously, we're gonna kill you. I'm done with this brute-force nonsense. I'm gonna look at every angle, work through all the details, and come up with a plan that'll put you down for good."

Outlandish as the statement was, his voice had been filled with unmistakable hatred.

Lily was the next to raise her hand. "What's this about a funeral?"

"The administration announced that they would be holding it four days from now. It's going to be a massive ceremony with guests from all across the world and over two thousand attendees. During the event, the boss's protection will be thinner simply by necessity."

Lily and the others had spent the last three days locked up, so all of this was news to them.

Prince Darryn's funeral.

The official position was that the killer had been located and no longer numbered among the living, so they wanted to hold the funeral as soon as possible. Prince Darryn had held a lot of international pull. The assassin's bullet threatened that, so Fend wanted to throw a huge event mourning him packed with foreign royalty and dignitaries in order to show the world that the Commonwealth was still strong.

Having another assassination take place there would demolish their reputation, and that was the one thing they absolutely couldn't afford.

Miné nodded. "Yeah, with big shots coming from across the world, you can bet that there'll be spies trying to worm through the cracks! Our counterintelligence teams will be working overtime! Ah-ha-ha, not that we have any responsibility to keep Bonfire safe in the first place!"

The CIM had no choice but to pull together the police and their domestic agents in order to guard against terrorism. In other words, it was going to be dead easy for White Spider to go after Klaus.

"Ohhh," the three of them said in understanding once they'd had it all spelled out for them.

There was no evidence that White Spider would actually come, of course, but it was far likelier than the odds of them stumbling into him while running aimlessly around the city.

"N-now that we have that figured out, we can come up with a strategy. You're a genius, Grete!" Lily grabbed Grete's arm and shook it up and down. "Let's bet everything we've got on the funeral and start making a plan!"

"There's just one thing...one big concern I have about after we find him." In contrast to Lily's, Grete's expression was downcast. "And if anything, it's the biggest problem of all..."

Her voice was grave. There was one piece of her analysis that she had yet to share with them.

"I'm worried about the way that people around him keep seeming to turn traitor."

Sure enough, Klaus's mentor Guido had betrayed Inferno—and White Spider was the one who shot him dead. White Spider was also the man who'd been manipulating CIM traitor Green Butterfly, and he was the one who'd hunted down Lamplight traitor Monika.

"For one, there are still a lot of questions around how Monika double-crossed us over such a short time frame."

"You're right. It all happened too fast," Sara agreed.

Not even the other Lamplight members had noticed that Monika was in love. The fact that someone had sniffed it out in an instant and leveraged it to make her turn traitor was a feat that took some genuine talent.

"Here's what I'm worried about."

Grete paused, hesitant to voice her concerns aloud.

"I fear that White Spider...may well have a unique ability to get his enemies to turn traitor."

""""————!!""""

The three girls' eyes went wide.

There was certainly a logic to Grete's deduction. There were people in Serpent's ranks with abilities that bordered on superhuman, like

Purple Ant and the way he took nearly three hundred normal civilians and transformed them into assassins. It made perfect sense that White Spider could have an ability that defied all common sense.

It was a soul-crushing realization to come to.

"What do you mean?" Lily asked, staring at Grete in shock. "Are you saying that someone else is going to double-cross us, too?"

Assuming that White Spider really did have that power, how had he used it to date?

By getting a member of the CIM's leadership to turn traitor, he pushed Belias to attack Avian and Lamplight.

By isolating Monika from the team, he'd forced her and Klaus into a duel to the death.

Those two betrayals had cost Lamplight dearly.

As the girls wrestled with this revelation, they noticed that Grete's hands were shaking.

"I'm scared… So scared I can't get to sleep at night…"

"Miss Grete?"

"If someone in the CIM joins Serpent's side, the boss's life will be in danger. I don't even want to imagine it, but…" Hesitant to speak the words aloud, Grete bit down on her lip, then bit it again. "…if they pump poison gas into the room he's being held in, then not even the boss will be able to do anything!"

It was all too easy to picture the scene.

Not only was Klaus wounded, but he'd been stripped of both his freedom and his weapons. Even he was only human. If he got sealed in a room with deadly gas, he would die.

Behind them, Miné scoffed. "A traitor in the CIM? Ah-ha-ha, that'd never happen!"

However, she was being overly optimistic.

"Please, you have to protect the boss…," said Grete. Lily was the closest to her, and Grete squeezed her hands in desperation. "I'm not a fool. I know that I would just make things worse if I left the hospital in my current state. So please, I'm begging you… Keep the boss safe in my stead…"

Tears spilled from her eyes and dropped onto her papers.

Grete had poured herself into those reams. She'd packed them full of countermeasures for every eventuality she could think of.

Then all the strength drained from her body.

"Miss Grete?!"

Sara hurriedly caught her before she could fall.

Grete had already fallen into a restful sleep, relieved that she'd done her part.

The girls didn't say much as they exited the hospital.

Seeing their wounded comrades had filled them with a renewed sense of responsibility, but it had also given them a keen sense of how much danger they were in. Once again, they were confronted with the reality of just how ruthless their foe was.

This was the man who'd destroyed Inferno by getting "Torchlight" Guido to turn traitor.

This was the man who'd secretly manipulated the CIM by winning over one of its leaders.

This was a professional assassin who'd already taken out Prince Darryn.

That was far from an exhaustive list, but even just those three were miracles beyond anything the girls would have been capable of achieving. It occurred to them now just how ignorant they had been to say that they were going to defeat him.

In the end, it was Sybilla who finally spoke up to try and raise their spirits. "L-look, at least we're not goin' in empty-handed here! Monika gave us that hint, remember?" She thumped Sara and Lily on their backs. "We've got code name Insight—the best pinch hitter anyone coulda asked for."

Before they set out for Fend, Lamplight had come up with a plan.

"Huh? Who's Insight?" Miné asked from behind them, but they ignored her. All of them had sworn not to reveal any information about Insight aside from their name.

Sara shook her head. "But even so, calling them in without a strategy won't do us any good."

They couldn't discuss details with Miné present, but Insight wasn't some superstar who could just swoop in and solve all their problems for them. They needed to devise a plan first, and they couldn't afford to put any more on Grete's shoulders.

"W-well, let's start by looking out for traitors!" Lily said. Her voice rang with anxiousness. "White Spider might try to get a new mole. Let's work together and try to find out what we can. If one of the CIM agents guarding Klaus changes sides, that'd be a disaster."

Grete had warned them to be wary of new traitors, and Lily had the right idea. That seemed like the logical place to start—

"Ah-ha-ha, you seriously think I'm going to let you go root around like that?!"

—but their babysitter Miné was having none of it. She let out another chipper laugh as she shut them down. "Like hell I'm going to let you poke and prod at our internal affairs when all you've got is flimsy speculation! The only job you handmaids have is to hunker down and not cause any trouble!"

".........!"

It boiled their blood, but they weren't exactly surprised. There was no way Miné was going to give them carte blanche to investigate whatever they wanted.

Sybilla shot Miné a scathing look, but that was the extent of what she could do. Considering their position, getting into a fight with the CIM would be foolhardy.

We don't have enough...

They were boxed in on all sides with no way out. They couldn't even figure out what the next move they needed to make was.

Not enough intel, not enough personnel, not enough talent, not enough anything.

White Spider's power was terrifying, and their time limit was tiny. They couldn't meet up with Klaus. The CIM members around them were being completely unhelpful.

But...if we keep dawdling like this, then what'll become of Miss Monika? What'll become of the boss?

Panic ran through Sara.

If they didn't capture White Spider, they couldn't save Monika.

If they didn't stop him, Klaus was going to die.

She understood all that, but she couldn't find a way forward.

The problem is, we don't have anyone we can turn to...

She clenched her fists in frustration.

As they stood there loitering helplessly in front of the hospital, Miné's radio buzzed. She had a message coming in.

After she held the radio to her ear and listened for a moment, her lips curled into a sneer. "Ah-ha-ha. I've got even more bad news for you."

She sounded oddly amused by the fact.

As for the girls, though, they'd had about all the bad news they could take.

"Oh, what a laugh. What was that you just said? Something about working together? Well, that's a pity! Turns out, your own teammates aren't interested in getting on the same page as you!"

Her tone was taunting. "What're you talkin' about?" Sybilla asked.

"It's killing time for me and the boys." Miné lifted the breast of her jacket to show off the gun holstered within. "'Forgetter' Annette just broke out of the hospital."

While Klaus and Amelie were in the middle of trading information, one of Amelie's agents came rushing in with a furious look on their face and quickly summarized the situation: "Forgetter" Annette had vanished from her hospital room.

The Lamplight girls were free to do whatever they wanted, but what they weren't allowed to do was to run around without their babysitters. According to Amelie's agent, all the CIM personnel in the area were searching for Annette.

For Klaus, the whole situation came as a surprise. He hadn't been allowed out to visit Annette in the hospital, so he had no way of foreseeing this.

He inhaled sharply. "...This is not good."

"No, it isn't." Amelie nodded. "It'll be a Vanajin unit that's tracking her down."

"I see. Well, you need to call them off."

"I know. Those people have a violent streak. If one of them ends up shooting Forgetter—"

"That's not what I'm worried about." Klaus needed to quickly clear up Amelie's misunderstanding. "I'm concerned that Annette will kill them all."

"I beg your pardon?" Amelie replied, but Klaus was being dead serious.

Klaus had predicted that losing to Monika would cause Annette to go feral. She'd never experienced a setback like that before, and there was an evil hidden away in her heart that made one's blood run cold. This was the first time she'd ever been given such a harsh catalyst, and the ensuing chemical reaction was liable to explode.

Now that he thought about it, perhaps Monika had been trying to bring out Annette's latent talent. However, the girl was such a black box that even Klaus was hesitant to poke too hard.

"What in the world even is that young lady?" Amelie asked. "She completely destroyed one of my men. With only one hand, Disintegrator Doll has been relegated to desk duty for the foreseeable future."

"Look, I made the call to make a forceful move."

Klaus was the one who'd given her the order to ambush the Belias aide, and Annette had accepted the assignment and completed it with ease. However, the really scary part was how she'd taken the severed hand and stomped on it with a smile on her face.

"But there's a lot even I don't understand when it comes to her."

That was the honest truth.

"All I know is that this world of ours is broken, and she's a person—a very scary person—who's adapted to that fact."

Some might describe her as being twisted to her core, but Klaus didn't want to use those words. However, it was hard to know what words *to* use to assess a girl who was willing to kill without hesitation or compunctions.

"You need to send Lily, Sybilla, and Sara after her posthaste."

"It sounds like that would be for the best, yes." Amelie nodded and quickly relayed instructions to that effect to her agent. Her ability to make quick decisions without needing a protracted explanation spoke to wisdom. "I take it the three of them know some method they can use to stop Forgetter. Just for my own edification, what exactly might that—?"

"Oh, they don't know anything."

"What?"

"I haven't told the girls about Annette's character yet. They have no idea how vicious she is."

"........." Amelie gave him a reproachful look. "Then how exactly do you expect them to stop her?"

She could glare at him all she liked, but Klaus stood by his call. It wasn't his place to thoughtlessly share Annette's private details. That was a decision he'd made not as a spy, but as her mentor. Annette herself had gone out of her way to keep her true nature hidden. Both when killing her mother and when attacking the problem customer at her restaurant job, she'd kept her teammates in the dark about what she was doing.

Klaus shook his head. "It's the only option we have."

It would be a different story if they were prepared to let him out of his room, but he knew better than to ask for that.

Amelie frowned, not at all convinced. "Are you sure you aren't placing too much trust in your subordinates?"

"Oh...?"

Amelie had spent a fair amount of time interacting with the girls. Perhaps her keen powers of observation had given her a cause for concern that Klaus hadn't picked up on yet.

"It's something I've been wondering for some time. You clearly think highly of your pupils, but have you forgotten what happened just the other day?"

"What are you talking about?"

"One of your students betrayed you. You failed them as a mentor."

Klaus had no rebuttal for the truth Amelie had just confronted him with. In failing to stop Monika, he had completely and utterly let her down, both as her boss and as her teacher.

"What I'm suggesting," Amelie went on, her tone still just as biting, "is that Monika's betrayal might very well be enough to break the girls' bonds."

◇◇◇

Annette's escape came as a huge shock to the CIM.

Not only had her arms and legs been bound, but because of the nature of the CIM-controlled hospital ward, its security was second to none. Sneaking in from outside and escaping from within both required a key and a special password. Unless you had a CIM escort, that was the only way you could get into or out of the building.

No one had ever escaped like that.

"Okay, first of all!!" Sybilla shouted as they raced down the streets of Hurough. "Is Annette even okay to be gettin' up and walkin' around?! I thought she was—"

"Supposed to be on strict bed rest, yeah!!" Lily shouted back. "But if anyone's gonna ignore that and just up and leave, it's Annette!!"

As soon as Miné filled them in, the three of them flew out of there like bats out of hell. After doubling back to the hospital to grab Annette's bedding, Sara gave it to her puppy so they could track Annette by scent. They knew she couldn't have gotten far from the hospital, so they narrowed their focus to the nearby alleyways.

It was still early afternoon at the moment, and the city was packed with people. One would imagine that a girl walking around in a hospital gown would draw a lot of attention. Despite that, the Lamplight trio couldn't seem to find her.

There were a couple reasons why they needed to track her down ASAP.

First off, the CIM had no patience for fugitives. There was a real danger they would do as Miné suggested and gun Annette down. Then there was the matter of how heavily injured she was. If her wounds got any worse, it could be life-threatening.

Miss Annette...

Sara turned her thoughts toward Annette's mental state and picked up the pace in impatience. Sara had made a big mistake, and she knew it. She regretted not having paid more attention.

As they continued through the crowd, the puppy running in front of Sara did an abrupt pivot.

"Mr. Johnny's picked up on something!"

The puppy in question bounded forward toward the entrance to a nearby piece of public infrastructure. It was facing the main road, but there was something unsettling about how dark it was, like an ominously gaping maw.

"It's the subway!!"

Hurough was home to the fastest metro system in the world. It had initially been built with steam locomotives that billowed smoke, but nowadays, those had been replaced with electric trains, and their tracks were spread all throughout the city.

"Clever thinking, Annette," Lily said as she sped up and charged inside. "She wanted to escape, so she went underground."

The stairs leading down were poorly lit, and the farther down they went, the more distant the sun's light grew. The ventilation system appeared to be working fine, yet the air grew thick and choking all the same. It felt as though the sooty air was going to wreck their lungs.

Surely, Annette wasn't actually going to get on the train.

When they got to the very bottom of the long staircase, they found a door marked STAFF ONLY. It should have been closed, but they could see that it was ever-so-slightly ajar.

The puppy nosed his way into the opening, and the girls followed along after him.

"These are the emergency tunnels," Miné said, sounding audibly impressed as she brought up the rear. The subway had walkways that ran parallel to the tracks designed to be used for maintenance or in case of accidents. Annette was taking advantage of that to get around.

The girls borrowed the emergency flashlights from the wall and hurried onward.

After a few minutes of running, Sybilla shined her flashlight on the hallway floor. "I see blood!"

Sure enough, there were red stains, dark enough that they were difficult to see without the light.

"Dammit, she knows she's not supposed to be up and about! She's probably keeled over somewhere down here—"

Right as Sybilla raised her voice, the subway train came blaring by. A terrible roar echoed through the hallway as a mass of metal thundered right next to the walls. The bright subway cars cast the entire walkway in light.

At the back of the group, Lily let out a small gasp.

There in the darkness, Annette was sitting on the ground with blood spilling from her lips.

Her back was resting against the concrete wall, and her eyes were closed. More dots of blood were dripping onto the ground.

"Miss…Annette…?"

As soon as the subway passed them by and the hallway grew quiet again, Sara called out.

"Your wounds have all opened up. We need to get you back to the hospital."

When she pointed her flashlight's beam at Annette, Annette's eyes snapped open.

She was alive. She'd been in better shape when she fled the hospital, but her condition must have deteriorated over the course of her escape.

Something about her feels different right now…

Sara gasped a little.

Without a moment's hesitation, Sybilla began heading over to her. "Hey, whoa, are you okay?"

When she did, Annette rose to her feet and swung something resembling a whip at the walkway floor.

Violent sparks lit up the maintenance passage.

"" ——!!""

Sybilla and Lily leaped backward. They bumped into Sara, who let out a cry as well.

In her hand, Annette was holding a thick electrical cable.

Not only had she stolen a knife, but she'd also used it to cut up the corridor's wiring. The live wire jutting out from within the insulation sent out small sparks as it short-circuited.

"Don't worry about me, yo."

This wasn't Annette's usual voice. It was completely devoid of emotion.

The sparks flying from the cable lit up her face as she stood there in the dark.

"I just need to go kill Monika real quick."

Sara felt a chill dance across her fingertips. Her breath caught in her chest, like she'd just been doused in ice-cold water.

The "Forgetter" Annette she knew always wore an innocent smile. As long as she didn't say too much, she came across as downright cherubic. She was an oddball, sure, and she caused more than her fair share of problems, but at the end of the day, she was an adorable girl whose very presence soothed their souls.

However, the being that stood before them now was utterly alien to Sara.

"Lily... Sara..." Sybilla's voice trembled. "She wasn't kiddin' just now... She's out for blood..."

She, too, had noticed that there was something wrong with Annette.

Sara and the others had always sensed that *something* was a little different about Annette. They'd spent enough time completing missions together to know that she was keeping some sort of secret.

However, none of them expected it to be something so extreme.

This was the side of Annette she never showed to the others—the fact that she got rid of anyone who dared hurt her. Even Monika.

Miné took a step forward and reached inside her jacket. She was about to pull her gun. "Wait!" Lily cried as she grabbed her.

They needed to talk Annette down, and fast. If they didn't, Miné would shoot.

"Miss Annette." Sara had the closest relationship with her, so she called out first. "Miss Monika is our friend, remember? I know she attacked you, but I'm sure she had a good—"

"What *is* a friend anyway?" Annette was unmoved. "You've never been more than playthings to me, yo."

"........."

"Don't get in my way. Just turn around."

A terrible feeling of emptiness struck Sara. It felt like someone was clamping down on her throat.

There were no falsehoods in Annette's words. All those times Annette had spent laughing and smiling with them, it had been because she enjoyed being there. Shallow concepts like emotional bonds had never been a part of it.

To her, anyone who drew her ire was a target for elimination.

It didn't matter if it was Klaus, or if it was Sara, or Sybilla, Thea, Grete, Erna, Lily, or Monika. If she didn't like someone, she was prepared to take their life without a second thought.

Hers was the ultimate case of egotism, yo.

There was a great evil inside her that she'd once kept hidden behind her angelic smile, and now it stood directly in their way.

Sara had no idea how to get through to her. They were at an impasse.

The first one to waver was Annette.

"Rgh!!"

Visibly pained, she swayed on her feet and spat up a mouthful of blood.

"Annette!" Sybilla cried.

As soon as she took a single step forward, though, Annette righted her posture and lashed out with her cable. Sybilla froze. Annette had no intention of letting them get anywhere near her. It was obvious that she needed medical attention, but she was uninterested in their concern.

Sybilla winced and shrank backward. With how linear the corridor was, not even her impressive reflexes would allow her to close that gap.

Lily bit her lip and took a step forward of her own. "Y-you know what, you're right. And I'm gonna help you kill her."

"The fuck?" Sybilla said with a look of shock.

Sara, on the other hand, picked up on what Lily was doing. She didn't actually mean what she was saying. Her plan was to offer empty promises to Annette in order to convince her to come back to the hospital.

"If you want to kill Monika, you're gonna need help. What do you say? Why don't we go get you patched up? You don't know where she is, right? I can help you look for her, so—"

"Spare me the cheap lies, Sis," Annette spat. "Do you seriously still think I'm just some dumb kid?"

"——!!"

Lily let out an ashamed gasp. The frigid, lightless void in Annette's eyes made it clear that her gambit was poorly chosen. Annette had dodged her dishonesty with ease.

"I don't get it, yo."

Annette cracked her electrical cable in frustration.

Sparks flew from the wires as they rubbed against each other, casting her face into stark relief against the darkness.

"I don't get why you're trying to stop me! What are friends even for? Why is it so wrong for me to kill people?!"

She swung the cable like a child throwing a tantrum, sending sparks scattering every which way. They flew against the ceiling, against the walls, and against the floor. The air itself was singed.

"Why am I different from everyone else?! Why do I keep having to hide that?!"

The sparks flew.

"It makes me feel trapped, yo!! Everything I see, I hate!!"

The sparks flew.

"When I grow up, will this red *redness* stop covering everything?!"

Redness?

Sara had no idea what to make of Annette's words. However, there was no sense trying to draw inferences from them. The world Annette saw was hers and hers alone. The rest of them had no ability to perceive it.

Annette was beyond their ability to comprehend.

She was trying desperately to tell them something. She was screaming out, revealing who she really was and fighting through her pain in order to get those terrible emotions out of her body.

However, Sara was powerless to do anything but stand there.

Beside her, Sybilla and Lily were in the same boat. All they could do was stare at Annette. And even if the rest of the Lamplight girls had been there, nothing would be different. Not even Thea with all her mastery of negotiation or Grete with her vast ingenuity would have been able to get through to Annette.

After all, how could you engage with someone whose only outlet for their impulses was murder?

"Ah-ha-ha, looks like you're out of ideas," Miné called dryly. "I'm not sure I totally follow, but that *thing* is out of its mind. Go ahead and stand back. I'll use Absolute Reverb to lock her down, then shoot her dead."

""No!"" Sybilla and Lily pleaded, but Miné simply arched her eyebrow. "What, you've got some idea for how to convince her?"

Upon seeing that the girls had no answer to that, she let out another one of her trademark laughs.

"You people are all talk." She gave them a toothy, mocking grin. "You say you're going to beat White Spider, but how're you planning on doing that, huh?! Go on, I'm waiting! Look at you people; you can't even talk down your own teammate! Ah-ha-ha, what a bunch of losers!"

Lily bit her lip. "........."

"You worthless little handmaids need to stay in your lane!"

Miné reached for her sonic orb, and Lily and Sybilla tried to stop her again.

Then they all heard a new set of footsteps coming from down the walkway. More CIM reinforcements. Once they got there, they were sure to back Miné up and attack Annette.

They had a deadline, and it was fast approaching.

If they didn't intervene, Annette and the CIM were going to murder each other.

I can't let that happen.

Fear swallowed up Sara's heart as she envisioned the worst-case scenario.

The way things were going, Annette was going to die.

However, the new problems that would arise if they helped her escape were self-evident.

I can't let Miss Annette die. I can't.

She needed to find a solution.

However, nothing Lily and Sybilla said had gotten through to Annette. All their attempts at mediation had ended in failure. The question was, who could converse with someone who existed outside the bounds of reason, who normal logic didn't apply to…

"——!!"

The moment it all clicked into place, Sara quietly sucked in a breath.

Her resolve was firm.

She began walking toward Annette and her electrical cable. After readjusting her newsboy cap, she sucked in another breath, this one big enough to fill her lungs all the way up. Sybilla and Lily urged her to stop, but she ignored them and kept on going.

"It's okay, Miss Annette."

She put on her very best smile.

"You don't have to be scared anymore."

For a brief moment, Annette opened her mouth in bewilderment.

That was all Sara needed.

"I'm code name Meadow—and it's time to run circles around them."

As she charged forward, she brought her full talents to bear.

Her animals had been hiding down on the tracks, and it was now that she gave them their orders. There was a hawk, a pigeon, some mice, and a dog—the full menagerie Sara had at her disposal. They leaped out of the darkness and moved to surround Annette.

"?!"

Annette was off guard, and she froze.

At that moment, Sara finished closing the gap. Annette tried to resist, but Sara slipped through her hands and pinned her from behind in an embrace.

"Everything's okay now."

She stroked Annette's head and hugged her tight.

"It's okay. It's okay, I promise! There's nothing to be afraid of."

"Get off me, Sis," Annette roared. "I'm not afraid, yo! I just don't get it, that's all!"

The nuzzling from all the animals must have really spooked Annette, as she'd already dropped her cable. She wriggled and squirmed to try to escape Sara's arms. It was incredible how strong she was when she was lashing out.

"I hate it! It makes me sick! It's so red! It's so red, and I hate it!"

Again, she was saying things that only made sense to her.

"You people are trying to trap me! To put me in a cramped little cage!"

Her rage was intense.

"And even if you don't! Someday, you'll start seeing me as a bad person and end up killing me!"

She was practically screaming, and she'd been doing so for so long that her voice grew hoarse. She gasped for air.

All the while, Sara continued hugging her without letting up.

"We're not going to put you in anything, Miss Annette!" she shouted back, her voice resolute. "Even if you're a bad person, and even if you kill people, that's no reason for us to reject you."

"Then what exactly do you want me to—"

"You don't have to change a thing!"

Sara touched Annette's cheek.

"No matter how bad of a person you are, I'll always accept you."

"What?" Sybilla and Lily yelped in bewilderment.

Sara didn't let up in her embrace. She bit down on her lip as though in prayer and refused to let Annette go. Her pets did the same, snuggling up to Annette and practically clinging to her.

The thing was, Sara knew.

She knew that when you were dealing with someone that words couldn't get through to, the first thing you needed to do wasn't to win them over. And it wasn't negotiating with or reprimanding them, either.

The first thing you needed to do was *affirm* them.

As soon as Sara realized that words weren't getting through to Annette, the answer came to her immediately. If anything, this was her area of expertise. She was the one who'd opened her heart to her hawk, her pigeon, her mice, and her dog, and she knew that you had to start by accepting them. You had to start by taking in every part of them. Getting them to answer commands was a problem for later.

That right there, that was Sara's specialty—the one thing she truly excelled at.

Slowly but surely, Annette stopped resisting.

"It…"

A faint whisper tumbled from her lips.

"It's okay for me to be a bad girl?"

"It's totally fine. You and me, we can find a way for you to keep being a bad girl together."

Sara gently brushed her hand through Annette's frazzled hair.

Eventually, Annette rested her weight against her. Before long, Sara heard the steady breathing of sleep. Her eyes were closed. Just like Grete earlier, her body had hit its limit.

Lily and Sybilla rushed over and let out loud gasps.

"She calmed down? For real?"

Miné's eyes went wide with disbelief at the radical transformation. She didn't know Annette well, so it was hard to blame her for her shock. When Annette wasn't raging, she looked like an adorable little angel.

That said, Sara had been treading on thin ice there. One wrong move, and Annette would have killed her.

She felt like she was burning up. Sweat cascaded down her body. Blood was coursing rapidly through her veins, and she didn't need to check her pulse to know that her heart was pounding a mile a minute.

Spurred on by her racing heartbeat, she spoke up.

"We're not worthless."

"Huh?"

"Please take back what you said earlier, Miné. You called us 'worthless little handmaids.' But we have someone who believes in us."

Sara stared at her, and Miné stared back blankly.

However, Sara wasn't actually mad at her. The only reason she'd been able to save Annette was because Miné's words had reminded her of something important she'd once been told.

"You have to figure it out. What sort of ideals do you have as a spy? How do you want to fight? What kind of life do you want to live?"

She held her second teacher in great esteem, and her second teacher had given her an assignment.

"Now I finally know what kind of spy I want to be."

Without averting her gaze from Miné, she spoke with conviction.

"I'm going to be Lamplight's guardian—a spy who never lets any of her teammates die."

Her mind was set.

To her, there was something more important than successfully completing missions or fulfilling her duty as a spy.

As she softly pressed her face against Annette's back, she took a moment to wonder how Monika would react if she heard Sara's answer.

Amelie's agent returned to the room Klaus was being held in and reported that Sara and the others had captured Annette. They'd just finished taking her back to the hospital.

"Good, they managed to stop her. Magnificent."

Klaus had little doubt that it was Sara who'd pacified Annette. Considering her ability to establish emotional bonds with animals that literally couldn't speak, all she would have needed to deal with Annette was a little courage.

As he breathed a sigh of relief, Amelie's expression soured.

"So everything went just as you planned, then, did it?"

She was a bit sore that her prediction had been off the mark.

"Not at all," Klaus said with a shake of his head. "And besides, you were absolutely right. I did fail as a teacher. I should have given Monika more of my attention."

"So you actually admit it?"

"Of course. But that doesn't mean that everything I ever did was a mistake." Klaus absolutely had some regrets about the ways he'd treated his subordinates, and his ineptitude still haunted him to this day. However, it was impossible to deny that the girls had grown tremendously. "And those girls are going to prove my worth as an educator."

That, he could say with confidence.

Klaus took pride in his role as their teacher. He was painfully aware of his own inexperience, but he always did the absolute best he could, and he knew better than anyone just how much those girls put into their training. Now they were going to go out and demonstrate the fruits of his tutelage.

Amelie adjusted her posture in her chair to compose herself. "You say that," she said, shooting him a stern look, "but as I mentioned before, I have some serious doubts about whether they're actually going to be able to defeat White—"

"It won't be easy, for sure. But aren't you overlooking something?"

Amelie blinked at him in confusion, and Klaus went on.

"I plan on putting White Spider in the ground, too."

He wasn't just going to idly sit around and leave all the work to the girls. That man had hurt Monika, he'd hurt Avian, and he'd hurt the girls, and Klaus was going to make him pay for it.

Then they heard a set of footsteps coming down the hallway, along with the jangling of jewelry clinking against jewelry. Klaus turned his gaze over to the door.

"And I imagine the CIM feels the same," he said. "Don't you want to take down the man who killed your prince?"

A response came from outside the room.

"Naturally. We at the CIM have no intention of letting Serpent off the hook."

After Amelie's agent freaked out for a moment, the door swung open.

"Mr. Nathan, sir!" Amelie said, hurriedly straightening her back.

Nobody had expected him to arrive quite so quickly.

The man standing there was in his midthirties and completely decked out in accessories. His hair fell all the way down to his waist, and between that and the bangles practically covering his arms, he made for a truly bizarre picture. The bangles had large jewels set in them, and every step he took caused them to let out a jarring cacophony.

"It's been a long time since we last met like this, Lone."

Hide was the group that controlled the CIM, one of the foremost intelligence agencies in the world—and "Cursemaster" Nathan was one of its members.

"Ah, so elegant…"

Klaus had no idea the man had found such success. "That was just the alias I was using at the time. Nowadays, I go by Klaus."

On hearing their exchange, Amelie's eyes went wide. "You and Bonfire know each other, sir?"

"We…ran into each other on a mission once. Some four years ago." Nathan rattled his bangles. "He was more violent then, and more beautiful."

"He's still plenty violent, I can assure you of that."

"No, he was far more unruly back then. Like a divine beast dispatched by God himself."

Four years ago, back when Klaus was working with his mentor Guido, they and a CIM team had gotten into a quarrel when they ended up going after the same target. Nathan and Inferno had fought alongside each other during the Great War, though, so they were able to settle the matter peacefully.

"I was sorry to hear about Hearth, Klaus. She and I met on a number of occasions. Her talent was so beautiful, it seemed like magic, and every time, I found myself captivated."

"Now's not the time to be bonding over the past."

As Klaus shook his head, the corner of Nathan's mouth curled upward. "No, I suppose it isn't."

At long last, Klaus finally had a chance to talk to someone in charge.

"Amelie," Nathan continued, "I'm sorry to ask this, but would you mind giving us the room?"

"...Of course. As you wish."

"I do apologize for the inconvenience, but I need you to get started on the thing we talked about."

For a brief moment, it looked like she was about to complain about being excluded from the discussion. However, she thought better of it and swiftly left the room.

The conversation they were about to have was highly confidential—enough so that they might need to fool their own agents about it.

As soon as the door closed, Nathan went on. "Now, this is you we're talking about. I take it you already have a plan in mind?"

"I have two," Klaus replied. "There's the excellent plan that'll be easy to pull off and requires next to no effort, and there's the terrible plan that'll be next to impossible to pull off and carries nothing but risks and costs. What one would you like to discuss first?"

Nathan's bangles jangled as he smiled. "How elegant."

Sara and the others saw Annette all the way to the hospital.

They couldn't afford to cause any more of a fuss than they already had, so calling an ambulance wasn't an option. Instead, they took whatever quiet back alleys they could find to transport their sleeping problem child. Miné handled the arrangements with the CIM.

Sybilla was the one carrying Annette on her back, and midway to the hospital, she spoke up. "You really sure about this?"

"Huh?" Sara replied from beside her.

"Y'know, all that stuff you said to Annette. Dunno how well that's gonna end..."

Sybilla was worried about what Sara had just said—that Annette didn't have to change, and that Sara would accept her no matter how bad she was. Assuaging Annette's fears had successfully ended her rampage, but thinking back now, those were some dangerous promises to make.

"O-oh no, I got carried away and accidentally said something outrageous, didn't I?!"

"You mean you didn't even think it through?!"

"I was desperate to calm Miss Annette down!" Sara replied with a nod. "B-but I'm sure it will all turn out okay."

As she said that, her hawk flew down from overhead and alighted on her hat.

Sara took off her cap and stroked the hawk's plumage. That was Bernard, her trustiest sidekick.

"You wouldn't know it by looking at him, but Mr. Bernard can be a pretty naughty boy. When he gets mad, he'll attack people even if I try to stop him. But he's still my partner." Next, she turned and stroked Annette's back. "That's why I know we'll find a way to handle Miss Annette, too, as long as that's what she wants."

"So she gets the same treatment as your animals, huh? But yeah, you're right. That's what you're so great at." Sybilla nodded in satisfaction and gave Sara a friendly pat on the head. "That's a good goal, bein' Lamplight's guardian. Knowin' you, you're gonna ace it."

"I'll be sure to do my best!"

Sara knew she was the one who'd said it, but hearing her own words again was still kind of embarrassing.

As she and Sybilla shared a smile, Lily piped up from behind them. "I still have one big question, though," she said, tilting her head and giving Annette a quizzical look. "How'd she manage to escape her hospital room in the first place? Wasn't she all tied up?"

"She most certainly was, ah-ha-ha!" Miné said. She was keeping a watchful eye on them all from the group's rear. "And why are you all acting like the case is closed? She gave us the slip and escaped our surveillance—that is a massive problem! You owe us." Her smile was the same as ever, but her eyes burned with rage. "I was right. We should've just kept you all locked up!"

She glared at them almost mockingly.

That was enough to drag the girls back to reality.

Nothing about their situation had changed. They still had no idea where White Spider was. They also suspected that he was an expert at getting people to turn traitor, but even if they wanted to work around that, the CIM was never going to let them go off on their own.

They needed more strength.

Now, to make matters worse, Miné was trying to restrict their freedom even more. She stomped over to Sybilla and began aggressively shaking Annette. "All right, out with it! How'd you escape the hospital? Answer me!"

Sybilla frowned and jumped away. "C'mon, don't wake her up."

However, the shaking was enough to rouse Annette from her slumber. "Hmnh…?" she grumbled, glaring at Miné in irritation.

Then she let out a barely coherent mumble.

"The Avian mask dude helped me break out, yo."

""""What…?""""

That was the last answer they'd expected, and the girls' eyes went wide.

"South Wind" Queneau stood outside Annette's hospital room.

Queneau was a large man wearing a white mask. He was an Avian member who, while taciturn, had remarkable technical skills. During spy missions, he mostly aided his team from the shadows through sabotage and assassinations. It was a role similar to Annette's.

After sneaking into the room, he quietly looked down at Annette atop the bed.

Annette was in pain. There was fury burning inside of her, and she lashed out in search of a target for it. The chains keeping her restrained clanged against each other. She couldn't undo them. She screamed and rolled onto her side. Try as she might to close her eyes and get some rest, though, the image of Monika manhandling her rose back to the forefront of her mind and sent her into a rage all over again.

"…Aye."

Queneau stared calmly at her agonized form.

"I ask you, chained Bloodfolk. Do you want to give in to your fury and destroy everything?"

He ran his hand over her chains.

Then, with a small nod, he pulled a scrap of metal out of his pocket and laid it on her pillow.

"Then go." He sounded a little forlorn. "This, too, is a ritual to aid your transformation..."

"Avian?"

The girls froze, their eyes still wide.

"South Wind" Queneau had given Annette a hand?

If they took her words at face value, that was what they implied. However, that was impossible. The man was gone. He'd died when Belias attacked his team.

Unsurprisingly, Miné burst into laughter. "Well *that's* obviously not what happened! Ah-ha-ha. We know perfectly well that everyone on Avian aside from Cloud Drift is dead and...dammit, you, don't go back to sleep! Get up!"

Having used the last of her energy, Annette returned to dreamland. She clung peacefully to Sybilla's back, undeterred by Miné's blustering.

Considering who they were dealing with, it was possible Annette had just been talking gibberish. Either that, or perhaps she'd been intentionally messing with Miné as revenge for having woken her up.

That was the logical explanation. It was the *only* explanation. The fact that Avian's members were dead was something that Lamplight had to accept.

However, Annette's nonsense gave Sara a clue.

A creature of legend sprang forth within her mind.

"...The phoenix."

Lily gave her a puzzled look. "Hmm?"

"Remember what we painted on the Heat Haze Palace wall? That symbol of Lamplight and Avian..."

A month prior, on the final night of Avian and Lamplight's shared honeymoon, the lot of them had partied until the wee hours of the morning, then painted a big picture on one of Heat Haze Palace's walls.

It was a picture of a phoenix.

One of them had suggested it, saying that it represented the unity of

Lamplight and Avian. The phoenix was an immortal bird out of myth, and they'd depicted it in the hopes that none of them would die, either. Strictly speaking, though, phoenixes weren't immortal. As the legend went, they charged into flames of their own accord when they reached the ends of their lives in order to be reborn.

That was what phoenixes really were—*birds that came back to life.*

"Look, what we're doing... This is the first and final joint mission between Lamplight and Avian. If we need more strength, all we have to do is borrow theirs!"

Fortunately, Miné's attention was focused on Sybilla and the girl on her back. When Sara explained her plan to Lily, she took care not to let Miné overhear.

"It's on us to resurrect Avian."

That right there was how they were going to beat White Spider.

The Lamplight girls were powerless, and Avian were the only ones who could lend them a hand. So it was time to accept some help—even if that help was coming from their fallen brethren, whom they would never get to speak to again.

Chapter 2

White Spider

Over at the CIM, preparations for Prince Darryn's funeral were proceeding apace.

This was Fend's chance to play itself up to forces both at home and abroad. It had taken them over ten days to capture the crown prince's killer, and the country had been in utter turmoil that whole time. Even now, the people still harbored some doubts about the government, the police, and their intelligence agency. The Commonwealth needed to demonstrate that it was unified and strong.

Ever since the United States of Mouzaia overtook them economically, the Commonwealth's international standing had plummeted. The royal family was their sole point of pride and the one thing they had over the United States. Queen Ribault was the leader of the entire Fend Commonwealth—the federation that had descended from the historied Fend Kingdom and its fourteen subordinate states—and the Commonwealth needed to reestablish the prestige the title carried.

This was going to be an event decked out with royals, world leaders, first ladies, and secretaries of state. Over two thousand state guests were going to attend the service in Shalinder Abbey, and the procession carrying Prince Darryn's body from the palace to the abbey was going to spend more than two hours traveling through the city. The Commonwealth absolutely couldn't afford to have any terrorism or riots take place during that time. They needed to crack down on malcontents and take preventative measures ahead of time.

The Fend government was doing everything in its power to prepare for the ceremony.

Meanwhile, Amelie, head of the Belias secret service unit, got a confidential set of orders.

Down in the CIM headquarters' underground interrogation room, Amelie took another look at her counterpart. The more she looked at her, the harder it all was to believe.

The other party couldn't have been older than a teenager. Based on her looks, she was more a girl than a woman. Her build was tall and slim. The prisoner's uniform she was wearing had short sleeves, leaving the crack-shaped scars on her arms visible and exposed.

A faint smile played at her lips, causing her jagged teeth to flit in and out of view.

This was "Magician" Mirena. She was a member of the CIM's Hide leadership. As the second daughter of the nation's third princess, she'd been assigned the post as per custom.

However, that wasn't the only name she had.

She also went by Green Butterfly.

Monika's knife attack had left her unconscious and in critical condition, but she'd finally recovered enough to hold a proper conversation.

Allegedly, she had thrown her lot in with Serpent. That intel had traveled from Monika to Klaus, then from Klaus to Amelie. It was a difficult accusation to believe, but the circumstantial evidence supporting it was overwhelming.

The idea that there had been a traitor in Hide would have been enough to shake the CIM to its core, and only a handful of Belias members and Hide themselves were aware of it. Nathan had ordered Amelie to carry out her interrogation in absolute secrecy.

Amelie was in there alone.

"Shall we begin, Ms. Mirena? Although I suppose I should call you Green Butterfly, now, shouldn't I?"

The two of them sat in the basement facing each other across a table.

"You're going to tell me everything. Every last detail about why you betrayed your homeland."

".."

The other spy didn't say anything for a good long while. She merely let out shallow breaths and looked at Amelie as though sizing her up.

"Let me out of here at once. You have the nerve to defy a member of Hide?"

"You aren't a part of Hide anymore." Amelie paid the veiled threat no heed. "Let us assume, for a moment, that you aren't a traitor. Even so, we failed to prevent Prince Darryn's assassination, we allowed Flash Fire to go on her rampage, and we have a whole host of injured agents. All of that can be traced back to the faulty intelligence you fed us—that hogwash about a spy team called Avian plotting to kill His Royal Highness."

"........."

"We are always just, and we do not err. The CIM has no need for personnel such as you."

All told, Monika dealt injuries of varying severity to over fifty of their operatives. Nobody ended up dying, but someone still needed to take responsibility.

Monika had taken her to the cleaners.

A jarring laugh made its way to Amelie's ears. "Ahhh, indeed. That will certainly do it. God*damn* do I hate the wretched masses."

A mocking, sadistic smile spread across Green Butterfly's face.

Amelie sucked in the faintest of gasps at the dramatic shift in ambience. "So this is you showing your true face?"

"Gee, it really is a shame. I mean, how incompetent can you people get? If Belias had just killed all of Avian like they were supposed to, this whole thing would've been over right then and there. You could've at least not given in to Lamplight the way you did. And how *stupid* do you all have to be to surround Monika with over a hundred agents and still have your arses handed to you?" Green Butterfly gave a devil-may-care shrug and let out another peal of scornful laughter. "You all were useless, and that's why I lost."

Amelie lashed out with her fist. She leaned all the way over the table and aimed her punch squarely at Green Butterfly's face.

Green Butterfly was too injured to even think about avoiding it.

"This is an interrogation room, not some place you can go running your mouth as you please. Know your place, you silly little girl."

The blow sent Green Butterfly stumbling backward. She fell on her hands and knees and clicked her tongue. "...Tch. Gee, why'd you have to go and do that?"

"I did some digging on you."

As Green Butterfly writhed on the ground, Amelie rose to her feet and sank her boot into Green Butterfly's gut. Each time she finished a sentence, she slammed her foot into the girl's body again.

"Your real name is Luehrs. You were born the second daughter of our third princess. But here in Fend, we have a custom of appointing one member of the royal family to help lead our intelligence agency. Records on you were erased, and you were trained to be an elite spy. You had to hold your post for thirty years, and until then, you were afforded no freedom. Yours was a cruel fate. But even so, you served your nation dutifully."

Once Amelie had finished covering every inch of Green Butterfly's body in bruises, she stopped her assault for a moment.

"I hear you were on good terms with Prince Darryn."

"...Yeah," Green Butterfly groaned. "You could say that. He was rather like an uncle to me."

Back in the day, that must have been incredibly useful for Hide. In Fend, having the royal family sign off on something opened up all sorts of doors. The royals had more clout than anyone, and having Green Butterfly act as a liaison between them and the CIM would have come as a massive help.

One day, though, all of that came crashing down.

"But you discovered His Royal Highness's secret, didn't you?"

"........................"

"And it was bad enough for you to sell your homeland out to the Galgad Empire. Am I wrong?"

None of that was more than conjecture on Amelie's part, but she framed it like a foregone conclusion, and her bluff paid off. The statements got a reaction out of Green Butterfly, albeit only a slight one.

"Well, hey." Green Butterfly's eyes widened. "Maybe you've got a head on your shoulders after all. Hee-hee. And here I was, thinking you were just another numbskull who wouldn't *dare* doubt her precious royals."

"………"

Not long ago, that had been true. Amelie had trusted the royal family, and she'd devoted her entire being toward serving Hide.

However, Klaus had given her a warning—*Question everything you know.*

She hadn't just blindly taken his advice, but losing to Lamplight and finding out about Green Butterfly had shaken Amelie's carefully constructed worldview and filled her with more regret than she could stomach.

Panting and gasping all the while, Green Butterfly used her trembling arms to slowly lift herself back to her feet.

Amelie's eyes went wide.

She'd attacked Green Butterfly viciously enough that she shouldn't have been able to move a single finger. Amelie had tortured over a hundred spies in her day, and not one of them had ever stood back up afterward.

"All I wanted was to share it!" Green Butterfly's lips quivered in pain. "Bad? Oh, it was bad. What I learned was just *wrong*. But no one believed me. They would never believe me. Even though he…he supported the Nostalgia Project! It was evil, and it drove me to despair. It was evil, plain and simple!"

Her voice had started out faltering, but by the back half of her speech, it took on a renewed fervor.

Eventually, she stood there on her own two legs and gave Amelie an intense stare.

"I thought I could split that despair with Monika. Gee, I really did. She was supposed to be my perfect partner."

"What's the Nostalgia Project?" Amelie had never heard of it before.

Green Butterfly spat out a mouthful of blood and gave her a grin. "You really want to know? Once I tell you, you'll never be able to unhear it!"

"………"

Amelie didn't like how forthcoming Green Butterfly was being.

There were parts of her attitude Amelie didn't at all care for, but they'd successfully established a dialogue, and Green Butterfly had revealed the name of the hitherto unheard-of Nostalgia Project all but unprompted.

She had an ominous feeling, but at the same time, turning back wasn't an option.

"I'm done being someone else's pawn," she replied. "I want to question everything, learn everything, and make my own decisions about how best to help my nation thrive. Now, tell me. *What was the nature of His Royal Highness's crime?*"

"Gee, I like that new look in your eyes."

Green Butterfly shot her a toothy grin and tottered back over to her chair.

Amelie returned to the table as well and sat down facing her.

"To explain the Nostalgia Project, there's a man I need to tell you about first."

"A man?"

"I met him two years ago. He's an absolute lowlife, and he came to me when I was in the depths of despair."

Green Butterfly went on, taking clear delight in watching Amelie's reactions.

"White Spider—the man who, for all intents and purposes, *built Serpent from the ground up.*"

While Green Butterfly's interrogation was going on, White Spider was working away at a typewriter in his hideout.

He'd just made a terrible discovery—their host had missed his deadline.

Resident cokehead novelist Diego Kruger had a contract with a publishing house. That publishing house wanted their manuscript, and they wanted it yesterday. *If you don't send it in, we're coming over there ourselves*, read the telegram.

That deadline had long since passed.

Having a third party show up at the apartment would be bad news for White Spider. However, Diego was deep in a narcotic stupor and unlikely to write so much as a page, and Black Mantis was out at the moment.

White Spider was left with no choice but to write it himself.

"This is a sick joke! Who the hell goes and starts moonlighting as a writer here at the eleventh hour?! I'll have you know I'm a very serious terrorist. I murdered a prince, for crying out loud!" he complained to no one. "This is BULLSHIIIIIIIIIIT!!"

But all his ranting and raving only echoed off the walls in vain.

Then a phone call came in from the publisher.

"Mr. Kruger, how's that manuscript coming along?! We're coming over right this minute!"

"Hi there, this is Mr. Kruger's assistant. Mr. Kruger is in the zone right now. If you interrupt him, I'll kill you."

White Spider briskly put down the receiver and let out a long sigh.

Welp, I guess I just gotta do this thing.

With that, he turned to the final resort of every writer who ever found themselves unable to advance their stories—plagiarizing his own life experiences without reservation or shame.

White Spider was once a soldier in the Galgad army.

He only joined up because it was impossible to find a decent job after the failed war, and he never put that much effort into his training. As a result of the peace treaty that they signed with the Allies after the Great War's end, the size of the Galgad Empire's military was strictly limited. On top of that, the army found itself under heavy criticism from the populace for having lost the war.

That was where he discovered he had a knack for long-range sniper marksmanship—but the era where a single sniper could change a war's tide had long since come and gone. None of his talent earned him much praise, and eventually, he got into a feud with a superior officer and found the whole thing so annoying he put a request to retire from the service.

From there, he spent his twenties unemployed.

It was the most freedom he'd ever enjoyed in his life.

Each night, he liked to buy a bottle of cheap beer and go lie down in a public park. There, lying on the unmaintained grass, he would gaze at the sky.

Y'know, the way things stand right now, I bet we're the weakest country in the world.

The night wind ran across his skin as he stared up at the steeples dotting the capital.

We got carried away and picked a fight with Fend and Lylat, got our asses handed to us, and ended up as the whole world's villains. They even took most of our colonies, so we're basically an empire in name alone at this point. And with reparations to pay that are dozens of times more than our national budget, we're basically the biggest losers around.

Law and order in the Galgad capital weren't much to speak of. As the wealthy made their riches off the recovery bubble and amused themselves with musicals and concerts, the underclasses spent their nights roaming the streets like wild dogs hunting for easy marks. In the parks, nights were defined by cash and booze, by drugs and sex.

Seeing the way the rich and the poor intermingled in the capital, it was almost like they were licking each other's wounds from the lost war.

He loved weakness, and he loved staring aimlessly up at the sky with nothing to his name but a few coins.

If a fight broke out, he always sided with the underdog. If he saw a man hitting a woman, he'd kick that guy across the road without a moment's hesitation. If he heard someone griping about their job, he would help them find a solution. Know who to fear. Know who not to—that was the creed he followed as he went around solving problems in his cowardly little way. Then he would pester the people he helped for some pocket change to support his homeless lifestyle.

He was the kind of layabout you could find just about anywhere in the world.

"What a coincidence. I love the weak, too."

One night, a middle-aged man showed up clutching a bottle of beer. He had the energy of a world-weary old man, and he took sparing sips from his high-proof beverage. His coat was tattered and dirty. The man's gut was worryingly flabby, and his hair had bits of white in it and looked like it hadn't been combed in ages.

The middle-aged man plopped himself down on the ground beside the young man, and the two of them began hitting it off as they shared drinks.

The younger man clapped his hands together. "You and me, we're cut from the same cloth."

The older man seemed tickled pink by the assertion. He covered his mouth with his hand and let out a booming "Ho-ho!" He was clearly a happy drunk, and a loud one. He took another swig. "But I have to ask, son, what is it *you* like about the weak?"

"I just like what I like. Who cares about why?" Still lying on the ground, the younger man smirked. "That's like asking why dudes love women with big ol' booties."

"Just give me the first thing that comes to mind."

"Okay, then it's 'cause I hate the way strong people act all high and mighty."

"Spoken like a true bum."

"You know I'm right, though. Think about how many people from other countries our military's killed. And think about how many of our people the Allies tore through."

"And you're saying that makes you mad?"

"All I know is, if every country in the world was equally weak, we wouldn't have to worry about wars. We could all just take a bottle of beer in one hand and our dicks in the other, and no one would have to die."

"Amen to that."

As they shared their casual back-and-forth, the older man paused for seemingly no reason and let out another booming "Ho-ho!"

The younger man plugged his ears with his fingers and grinned. Trading meaningless banter with complete strangers was one of his absolute favorite ways to kill time.

However, the next thing the older man said caught him by surprise. "The Weakest Problem Solver in the Capital."

"Huh?"

"That's what they call you, isn't it? A stray dog who only accepts tiny payments for his services, who has no friends or property or home to call his own, and who has nothing to lose? I must say, you're a pretty odd duck."

The younger man blinked. Apparently, his new friend already knew everything about him. However, he wasn't too bothered by that. After all, he was drunk.

The older man thumped him on the shoulder. "My boss has taken a fancy to you. Ho-ho. I'd love to arrange a meeting, if you'd let me."

He raised his bottle aloft.

"There are people trying to violate the world you love so dearly. What do you say we save it together?"

Then he introduced himself.

The portly middle-aged drunk had a name—and that name was Indigo Grasshopper.

The younger man's head was muddled from the booze, and he largely assumed that Indigo Grasshopper was joking. After all, he was dealing with a jolly old middle-aged drunkard who was saying crazy shit like "We're a group called Serpent" and "We're spies who travel across the world" with breath that reeked of alcohol. Every so often, Indigo Grasshopper would pause to howl "Ho-ho!" up into the night sky. There was no way the young man was going to take him seriously.

"Follow me," Indigo Grasshopper said, and the two of them walked through the city. The younger man had no idea where they were going, but he was excited to find out.

As it turned out, their destination was the Galgad Ministry of Defense building.

Holy shit, the younger man thought.

All the lights inside were off. "I got a member of parliament to clear the building," Indigo Grasshopper said as if it were no big deal. After using a passkey to go through the back entrance, Indigo Grasshopper headed to a locker room. It was clear from watching him that it wasn't his first time there. He retrieved a suit jacket from one of the lockers and cast off his ratty coat.

At that point, the younger man started sobering up in a hurry.

"Allow me to introduce you." All of a sudden, Indigo Grasshopper's voice was far more collected. "This individual is Serpent's boss."

The person in question was waiting for them in one of the ministry's offices.

The moment their gazes met, the blood drained from the younger man's face, and he found himself holding his breath. He could tell that he was looking at something that ought not be seen. It was the first time in all his life he'd felt that way.

That still, oppressive pair of eyes never released him from their sight.

Indigo Grasshopper handled all the explanations. In a much more serious tone than before, he explained that there was a plan called the Nostalgia Project being carried out in secret, that Serpent was an intelligence unit trying to stop it, and that they operated independently from Galgad's traditional intelligence structures.

None of it sounded remotely believable.

When the younger man faltered, Serpent's boss opened their mouth.

"*The Nostalgia Project's goal,*" they said, their voice gravelly, "*is to eradicate the weak from the world.*"

That was all, and from there, Indigo Grasshopper resumed his explanation. He showed the younger man proof as well; he had photos and voice recordings to back up everything he was saying.

Just hearing the details of the Project was enough to make the younger man's blood run cold. Even with the most conservative estimates possible, the casualty count would still number in the millions. It would be a black mark on human history. Every fiber in his body was screaming that it needed to be stopped. When Indigo Grasshopper told him that people were trying to violate the world he loved so dearly, he hadn't been exaggerating.

At the same time, though, he immediately understood just how difficult the Project would be to impede. Doing so would require putting pressure on influential parties across the world, but if they did that, it would mean going head-to-head with other intelligence organizations.

"O-okay, wait, hold on now! I'm picking up what you're putting down! I believe you, I do!"

"Ah, what a comfort to hear," Indigo Grasshopper replied. "Looks like you've got a good head on your shoulders. And here I was, afraid you might dismiss me as a conspiracy theorist—"

"Yeah, yeah, thanks. But there's one thing I don't get."

"Hmm?"

"What do you want *me* to do?"

Spittle flew from his mouth as he wailed.

Everything they were talking about was way above him. His knees were rattling, and he couldn't make them stop.

"This doesn't make sense. Serpent's this spy org that's gonna turn the world on its head, right? What's a badass team like that want with a guy like—"

"We want you to recruit for us," Indigo Grasshopper replied.

"Huh?"

"The boss can tell you've got a knack for it."

Then, without a shred of embarrassment, he laid out the truth.

"And right now, Serpent only has two members. It's just me and the boss."

"The *fuck*..............?"

The young man froze with his mouth hanging open.

Upon seeing his shock, the two members of Serpent gave him a pair of self-deprecating shrugs.

At that point, the sheer hilarity of it all began hitting him. With little regard for the fact he had an audience, he clutched at his chest as side-splitting laughter started bubbling up from the deepest parts of his gut. "Ha-ha-ha-ha, ahhh-ha-ha-ha! You're serious? You're actually serious?! You guys?! The two of *you* are gonna take on the biggest intelligence agencies in the world?! How do you think that's gonna go for you, huh?!"

Indigo Grasshopper gave him another shrug. "You're not wrong."

"You know what, boss? I like you. And you, too, Indigo Grasshopper.

I can never say no to a good underdog story." He wiped a tear out of the corner of his eye. "And hell, Serpent's gotta be the weakest spy team in the world."

Eventually, the shocked nations of the world would come to perceive Serpent as an intelligence unit shrouded in mystery—a mighty organization they knew nothing about, one completely divorced from the conventional Galgad Empire structures.

However, that was a far cry from what it actually was.

In truth, it was a tiny intelligence team that three people had built the way one would a start-up company. The average detective agency had a larger staff than they did. That was why it was so hard to track down.

It was just three people—three people against the world.

Serpent's boss gave the young man the name White Spider, and Indigo Grasshopper taught him the basics of espionage.

According to them, they'd seen a talent in him—the ability to love people's weaknesses.

He was the kind of guy who would sling an arm around a pauper's shoulder and unashamedly laugh, "Look at us, just a pair of broke bums." The kind of guy who would go to someone with a broken heart and sob, "I want a girlfriend, too!" The kind of guy who would find someone getting ground down by workplace drama, say, "I feel you, man," and mean it from the bottom of his heart. He could identify people's weaknesses without even talking to them, and it was in his nature to genuinely empathize with them.

"Don't think of it as trying to recruit the best spies; think of it as looking for drinking buddies you feel like you would hit it off with," Indigo Grasshopper told him. "That's probably the best way to make use of your skills."

"You make it sound so easy," White Spider replied, then scratched his head and agreed to go along with the plan even though he only sort of meant it. "But look, man, if I go around collecting people I get along with, we're gonna end up with a bunch of crackpots. You know, the kind of weirdos that don't play well with others."

"That's absolutely fine." Indigo Grasshopper gave him a big nod. "If anything, so much the better."

In the end, White Spider spent the next several years rubbing shoulders with people from intelligence agencies all over the world in search of personnel.

Just as the other two had predicted, his efforts ended up paying huge dividends for the team.

From the United States of Mouzaia's JJJ intelligence agency, he got the Qiongqi—later known as Black Mantis.

White Spider started out as a spy visiting the Galgad Empire.

The Empire's Ravine intelligence agency had been keeping an eye on the Qiongqi for a while. The man cared more about renovating his prosthetics than his actual missions, and he embezzled money that came from his homeland to buy new parts. Every so often, he remembered to send fake reports back home, and when he did, he always demanded more money. "I'm about to make a breakthrough," he would tell them.

The man was obsessed with his prosthetics, and White Spider found that positively endearing.

"Let me guess—you wanna be a hero, don't you?" he said one day, stopping by the Qiongqi's hideout. "But they never give you any decent missions, so you content yourself with conning your allies and languishing away. Gotta say, that's pretty pathetic."

The man shot him a murderous stare. "And who the hell are you?"

White Spider shrugged. "A guy even less cool than you."

It only took White Spider a few short conversations to get the Qiongqi to drop his guard, and once he explained the Nostalgia Project, the man decided to join Serpent. He was a tall man who never removed his hood, and he casually brandished his three right arms.

"Ah, finally someone recognizes my potential. Perhaps this is fate."

From the Bumal Kingdom's Curse intelligence agency, he got Breeder—later known as Silver Cicada.

The next spy White Spider found was a woman about his age.

Breeder had had doubts about her intelligence agency from the get-go. She was disillusioned with its constant choices that served no purpose but to curry favor with the fat cats in charge of their government, and she didn't believe in the administration enough to risk her life for it. She made sure to keep her feelings hidden from her colleagues, but she couldn't escape White Spider's eye.

He gave her his pitch in front of a politician's estate. "Man, I feel you. Personally, I make sure to find some jackass politician's car every morning so I can stick a wad of gum on it."

Breeder didn't hesitate a moment. She made her decision fast and immediately agreed to join Serpent.

"I owe you a deep debt. Never before have I had a compatriot who saw things as I did. Please, allow me to pledge my allegiance to you."

Her hair was tied up in a colorful hairband, and she assassinated the politician she was supposed to be guarding before making a bold declaration.

"I am Silver Cicada! Now behold, as I sully my homeland and purge the world of the maggots infesting it!"

From the Lylat Kingdom's Genesis Army intelligence agency, he got Deimos—later known as Purple Ant.

White Spider only came to know him by a lucky stroke of fortune. Over in the United States of Mouzaia, Deimos attacked him, then took an interest in him. That said, Deimos taking an interest in someone simply meant wanting to hear their dying words. Rather than kill White Spider on the spot, he decided to instead torment him first, then kill him later.

The man who'd tied White Spider up and was delightedly harassing him with a stun gun was thin and had a gentle face. White Spider sensed such violent urges in the man that it made his hair stand on end. However, he could tell that there was something keeping the man's repugnant power in check.

Getting him to come around took a good long while.

"I'm afraid I'm not interested," Deimos told him. "Though I will admit that I don't much care for the way those Allied bastards are living it up while much of the Western-Central world is still reeling from the horrors of war."

"Look, from what I've seen, you've made a couple slaves for yourself." White Spider gave him a provocative grin. "But you wanna really go wild, don't you? What, did Nike order you to hold back or something?"

The name he dropped was that of a world-famous spy—Nike, the strongest counterintelligence agent in the Lylat Kingdom.

There wasn't a person in their line of work who hadn't heard her name. She was a legend, and it hadn't taken White Spider long to figure out that she was the one holding Purple Ant's leash. Purple Ant was such a monster that no one but Nike could have possibly controlled him.

"C'mon, let your instincts run wild. You wanna tear everything down—and I get that."

White Spider didn't flinch; he just kept on throwing words at the terrifying being before him.

Eventually, Purple Ant signed on.

"Maybe you're right. I guess ruling over Mitario as its king might be kind of nice."

For two whole years, White Spider continued gathering members for Serpent.

Considering that he'd been unemployed up to that point, the results he put up were nothing short of miraculous. However, White Spider had no idea that his work had attracted some unwanted attention.

That attention led to a meeting—one that would prove to be a major turning point for the team.

It was the day that all of Serpent was going to gather under one roof for the first time.

White Spider had surreptitiously sent word to all the members, and he made his preparations to introduce them all to Indigo Grasshopper and the boss. He was the one who'd handled the communications, who'd arranged to smuggle everyone into the country, and who'd put plans in place to fool their respective intelligence agencies. He figured that rather than telling each of them their agenda separately, it would be more efficient to get them all together and do it in one go.

That was a fatal mistake.

There was no need to bring every member in the org together like that, and if he'd told Indigo Grasshopper about his plan ahead of time, Indigo Grasshopper would have stopped him on the spot. However, White Spider's string of successful recruitments had both gone to his head and left him exhausted, both of which dulled his judgment and led him to his folly.

They gathered on neutral ground. It was a mountainous nation not far from the Empire.

White Spider's schedule that day was packed. In the afternoon, he went to the airfield to greet Purple Ant.

"Excellent, Spider. Very good. A king deserves a kingly welcome." When he got off the airplane, he did so with ten slaves in tow. "For your reward, I'll punish you—by killing you thrice over."

"How does that make any sense?!"

That evening, he got a call from Black Mantis saying he didn't want to come.

"A soothsayer told me my fortunes were bleak. It might be time for me to retire."

"Just get your ass over here already!!"

When night fell, he met up with Silver Cicada in an alleyway by the station and learned that she'd gotten herself into trouble.

"Mr. Spider, sir! Last night, I lost all my operating funds at a casino—"

"I'll spot you!"

His teammates were giving him one headache after another.

Wait a minute, am I basically at the bottom of the Serpent pecking order?

He should have had seniority over all of them, yet you never would have guessed from the way they treated him. He didn't like that realization one bit, but he continued doing his prep work all the same.

From what he'd heard, the boss and Indigo Grasshopper were hiding in a villa located on one of that nation's outlying islands. He didn't know the details, but for some reason, the boss needed to constantly change their whereabouts.

It was only when the four of them—White Spider, Black Mantis,

Silver Cicada, and Purple Ant—reached the harbor that White Spider realized the depths of his blunder.

"Well, well, well. What a fun little group we've got here."

There was a man lying in wait for them.

He was sitting in their boat wearing a navy-blue jacket and an easygoing smile. Swords were a weapon hardly befitting a spy, yet there was one resting on his shoulder all the same. Despite his stately beard, the jovial grin on his face made him come across as unserious.

"The Qiongqi, Breeder, and Deimos, huh? You've got a good eye on you. Pretty impressive, how you managed to assemble a bunch of spies that my boss was *already keeping tabs on*." The sword-wielding man slowly rose to his feet. "What're you plotting, mushroom-head?"

White Spider couldn't move. He could barely even feel his own legs.

Indigo Grasshopper had given him the rundown on the basics of the espionage landscape, so he knew that there were two people whose combat skills were wholly unmatched. The raw violence they commanded was the pinnacle of what mankind could achieve, and no one could ever hope to beat them in a fair fight. If one of them came at you, your only options were fleeing or conning them. Fighting back was a surefire route to an early grave.

There was Nike, the Lylat Kingdom's lady of the hammer who ruled over and protected its capital. And there was Torchlight, the Din Republic's swordsman and Inferno's second-in-command.

Now the latter of the two was giving him a probing look.

White Spider couldn't sense a single bit of bloodlust or fervor from him. He'd clearly noticed the four of them, but he wasn't letting any of his hostility show.

"It's four against one, Mr. Spider," Silver Cicada crowed. She clearly had no idea who the man was. "I say we slaughter the knave!"

She pulled out two fistfuls of syringes and rushed the swordsman down.

Once she went in, the rest of them had no choice but to follow up. White Spider drew his pistol, and Black Mantis brandished his prosthetics and rushed after Silver Cicada with a cry of "Surmounters, avail me!" As they did, Purple Ant gave an order to his ten subordinates. **"Tear him apart."**

The swordsman—"Torchlight" Guido—slowly reached for his sword's handle.

Then the world *ruptured.*

White Spider couldn't think of any other way to describe it. As soon as Silver Cicada and Black Mantis got close to Guido, they went flying like they'd just been blasted away by an invisible explosion. Black Mantis's prosthetics and Silver Cicada's syringes shattered into pieces, and lacerations shot across the bodies of Purple Ant's men and splattered their blood across the ground. Meanwhile, the bullet White Spider fired simply vanished into thin air—or at least, it appeared to. In truth, Guido had sliced it to bits.

By the time White Spider finally understood what had happened, Guido had already closed in on him. White Spider tried to hit him with the butt of his gun, but his efforts were in vain, and Guido hit him and Purple Ant with the flat of his sword in rapid succession. When a blow smashed White Spider in his left arm, the arm twisted backward like all its bones had vanished.

Not even two seconds had passed, and the situation had completely unraveled.

Not a single one of the spies White Spider had gathered were still on their feet. They'd been fighting so boldly just moments before, but now they were lying unconscious on the ground to a man. Guido had completely annihilated them.

"That's it, huh?" Guido said. He swung his sword to shake off the blood. Then he turned his disappointed gaze over to White Spider, who was cowering on his knees. "Now, as for you—"

"Ah..."

White Spider had been too befuddled to do anything, but now he understood the situation clearly. He was about to die. Guido was going to torture him, make him give up every bit of intel he had, then lop his head off once he was finished. There was no way White Spider could escape from a titan like him. He trembled from head to toe, and tears welled up in his eyes. His body felt like it was burning up and freezing over at the same time, and the urge to vomit was overwhelming.

He needed to pull Guido onto his side.

There was no other way for him to survive. However, he didn't have enough time left to suss out Guido's weaknesses.

At that point, the only thing driving him was a primal desire to live.

"Please, just spare my life."

Guido scrunched up his face. "What?"

"I'll do anythiiiiing! I'll kill whoever you waaaant! If you want money, just name your price! I don't wanna diiiiiiiiiiiiiie! Waaaaaaaaaah!"

He screamed. He wailed. He sobbed. He cast aside every ounce of pride he had and poured everything he had into begging for his life. For all the allies he'd gathered and all the achievements he'd let go to his head, all he could do in the face of such might was to brownnose, lick the man's boots, and debase himself in every way possible.

"This is buuuuuuuuuullshit, man! How am I ever supposed to beat youuuuuuu?! Damn you, Indigo Grasshopper, you tricked meeeeeeeeeee! I'll get you for thiiiiiiiiiiiis!"

To top it all off, he even started badmouthing the people who led him to that point. He spent the next little while shouting about how Serpent's boss and Indigo Grasshopper needed to "eat shit and die," then choked on his own spit and lapsed into a coughing fit.

Then he realized something.

"...I think I soiled myself."

There was a foul odor coming from his lower body.

"...And I think it's number two."

Guido grimaced.

Snot and tears rolled down White Spider's face as he went on. "Please, oh high and mighty Torchlight, I'm begging you." Still down on his knees, he bowed low. "You have to at least hear me out."

It was the most pathetic pleading anyone had ever done. Guido had seen hundreds of people beg for their lives over his long career as a spy, but that was the worst demonstration he'd witnessed by a country mile. The way the weakness-loving White Spider had abandoned any semblance of pride had been truly disgraceful.

At the end of the day, though—*doing so had been the right call.*

If he'd gone for some sort of half-assed bargaining, Guido would have sliced off his arms and begun the interrogation without a second thought. Being a spy demanded ruthlessness, and that was something Guido certainly had. However, he'd stayed his hand.

Only a man who truly loved weakness and was loved by it in turn could have been unsightly enough to make that happen.

Guido let out a small sigh. "Now I don't even *want* to kill you." With that, he stowed his sword in its sheath.

Guido gave White Spider a scathing glare. "I've never even seen someone beg that appallingly." But White Spider was downright pleased. The way he saw it, the fact that he was still alive meant that whatever he'd done, he did it perfectly.

However, he did end up having to reveal every bit of Serpent intelligence he knew. White Spider had no interest in protecting classified information when his life hung in the balance.

When he got to the bits about the Nostalgia Project, Guido didn't seem particularly surprised. He simply scowled a bit and said, "Yeah, I figured." Apparently, Inferno already had some preliminary intel on it.

"If what you're saying is true, then I gotta go talk things over with my boss," Guido said. "Out of respect for that repugnant begging you did, I won't kill you just yet."

He sounded supremely confident, and he even left the other three alive, too. After tying up their hands and legs, he locked them in an abandoned house and freed the people Purple Ant had brought.

There was no one guarding them. Guido hadn't brought any of his teammates along.

When White Spider realized that, he let out a grim laugh.

Not only had "Hearth" Veronika caught wind of everything he'd been doing, but she'd also determined that it would take a single agent to bring him down. Then "Torchlight" Guido had gone and completed the mission without breaking a sweat like the avatar of violence that he was.

How the hell did he get it in his head that he could go up against people like that?

Even after they were awake, Purple Ant and Black Mantis didn't say a single word. The two of them were prideful, and they were taking their crushing defeat hard. Silver Cicada, on the other hand, was the picture of cheer. "This house reeks, doesn't it?" she noted.

One way or another, this is curtains for Serpent.

Now that they were in Inferno's crosshairs, they were doomed. Any moment now, Guido would return with his teammates in tow to capture Serpent's boss and Indigo Grasshopper.

I hope the boss and Indigo Grasshopper manage to escape, but I don't love their odds...

The detainment continued for nearly a week. The good news was, Guido had hired some locals to look after them.

The next time Guido showed up, he looked haunted. His face had the telltale pallor of sleep deprivation, and considering how haggard he was, he probably hadn't been eating much, either. It had only been a week since they saw him, yet he looked like a completely different man.

White Spider braced himself for death all over again. The coldness in Guido's eyes was that of a man about to carry out an execution.

However, nothing could have prepared him for what Guido was about to say.

"The boss and I are through."

White Spider froze in shock, unable to process what he'd just heard.

Could Inferno's boss Hearth really have had a falling-out with her second-in-command Torchlight? What could have happened between them?

"Why's it gotta be like this? Damn it all...," Guido groaned. Blood dribbled from his tightly clenched hands. White Spider didn't even want to think about how much force a person must have to squeeze down with to make their nails break their own skin.

"I wanna talk to your boss, mushroom-head."

Then Guido delivered another unexpected message.

"I'm joining Serpent."

◇◇◇

Not even White Spider had seen that betrayal coming.

From the Din Republic's Foreign Intelligence Office, he got Torchlight—later known as Blue Fly.

For Serpent, getting Guido was a massive boon. On his suggestion, Purple Ant returned to Mouzaia's capital and got to work reinforcing his army. Once its ranks hit the two hundred mark, he selected the finest among them and put together a team of unparalleled assassins. On top of that, Purple Ant had always had a soft spot for "Deepwater" Roland, but now he began really putting Deepwater to work.

One thing Purple Ant did was lend him to the Galgad Empire's main intelligence agency in order to build up Serpent's relationship with them. Indigo Grasshopper had always been hesitant to get too close with the rest of Galgad's intelligence community out of the fear of leaks, but even he signed on. "If Guido says it's the play, then we'd best follow his lead."

There was one person who benefitted immensely from their newfound financial support from the Empire, and that person was Black Mantis. Through a series of alterations, he was able to build a pair of prosthetics that boasted power beyond anything the human body was capable of. Their mechanical limitations meant that they had limited uptime, but in short bursts, their combat potential was on par with Guido's.

In just a short half year, Serpent had advanced by leaps and bounds.

Thanks to Guido's coaching, Silver Cicada's assassination techniques had improved dramatically. Getting lessons from one of the top spies in the world seemed to be bearing fruit, and she often cried, "He's incredible, he really is!"

Guido gave White Spider some pointers on occasion, too.

"You know what your problem is? You're petty and small-minded, and you always will be."

"Surely there's gotta be a nicer way you coulda put that!"

Guido had to pull the wool over Hearth's eyes every time he got in touch with Serpent, but he still found the time to teach them a number of combat techniques and gave them instructions to practice on their own time.

"But hey, maybe that's fine. Maybe the world could use a spy like that," Guido said with a laugh from his Fend Commonwealth hideout. "After all, it's that weakness of yours that drew all of Serpent's members to you."

"C'mon, you're giving me too much credit. I was just running around doing my job, and—"

"Nah, you're the one who built Serpent."

White Spider had no idea what Guido was talking about. However, Guido sounded like he meant what he was saying. "Indigo Grasshopper agrees with me. He said that you're the heart and soul of the team," he continued, his voice dead serious.

White Spider let out a small grunt as his face went red with embarrassment. He still thought of himself as nothing more than a lowly peon, and that really was all he'd been trying to do.

"But what you don't have is the conviction."

"Huh?"

"Being a spy is all about warping the status quo. Fighting back against this world awash with pain and really changing things takes a certain mindset, and you don't have the conviction for that." Guido pressed the back of his blade against White Spider's chest. "Remember this: The team we're about to kill, Inferno, *is* the status quo."

White Spider raised an eyebrow.

None of what Guido was saying really made sense to him. Rather than offer him any further explanation, though, Guido's voice simply hardened. "Let's go."

That was Serpent's first mission—eliminating Inferno.

Indigo Grasshopper was the one who made the call. If they didn't take down Inferno, then Inferno was going to wipe them out.

Guido was the one who handled all the planning. Inferno's members were scattered across the globe. His plan was to lay traps for each of them in turn, and Guido laid out all their locations and weaknesses.

Guido and White Spider's target was "Firewalker" Gerde, the invincible elderly sniper. In order to take her down, the first thing White Spider did was find them a new teammate.

From the Fend Commonwealth's CIM intelligence agency, he got Magician—later known as Green Butterfly.

With that, Green Butterfly became the team's newest spy. She had ugly suspicions about her nation's royal family, and White Spider got close to her to get her to flip on them. However, she was so arrogant that White Spider knew he needed to take her down a peg, so he conspired with Guido to do just that.

Just as he planned, Gerde wiped the floor with her.

As Green Butterfly lay bleeding from the shoulders on the dance hall floor, Gerde pressed a foot against her spine and a rifle against the back of her head. Green Butterfly let out a wail of pain.

"Hot damn, you got your clock cleaned *good*."

When White Spider walked in and let out a derisive laugh, Green Butterfly glowered at him. "Oh, shut the hell up… What are you even doing here?"

He chuckled and gave her an unapologetic shrug. "This was a test. You're too cocky. Word to the wise: When you're a small fish, you gotta keep your head down."

Green Butterfly gave him an absolutely murderous glare, but White Spider ignored her. There was someone he needed to be far more worried about. "Firewalker" Gerde was holding her rifle and staring his way with a look in her eyes that said she was just itching for a fight. Her tank top left her arms all but bare, exposing the muscles bulging from them like armor. In no world did she look like a woman in her seventies. Her face had the wrinkles typical of someone her age, but the aggression lurking in her eyes was that of a much younger woman.

The person she was looking at wasn't White Spider—it was the man beside him, Guido.

"Oh, huh. So you're here, then, are you?"

"Yeah. Yeah, I am. Sorry about this, Granny G."

From the outside listening in, one could have mistaken their conversation for a pleasant chat. Peaceful as their words were, though, the air was so rife with tension White Spider could feel it in his skin. He couldn't close his eyes. He knew that if he blinked, it might well be the last thing he ever did.

His job there was to observe. Indigo Grasshopper had ordered him to make sure that Guido didn't rejoin Inferno's side. Personally, White Spider found the whole notion absurd. Even if Guido and Gerde did start colluding, what the hell was *he* supposed to do against those two monsters?

The tension between the two master spies mounted—

"Welp, guess this here's the end of the line."

—but Gerde was the first to loosen up.

She tossed her rifle on the ground. "I know when I'm licked. I can't beat you, not when you're already this close."

"You sure? I was rarin' to go."

"Ten years ago, I would've given you props for saying that. Then I would've laid you out on your punk ass."

Gerde took the chair that had gotten knocked over in the middle of the dance hall, stood it back up, and sat herself down in it. Her posture was impeccable, and her back was as straight as an arrow.

Guido sensed what she was getting at and went to stand across from her.

"..............."

He looked down at her. His sword was still stowed in its sheath. He just stared at her, so motionless it was like he'd forgotten how to move his body.

"The boss came and cried to me in secret. It killed her that you couldn't see things her way," Gerde said. Her voice was gentle now, a far cry from the severity she'd been showing to date.

"She was really that torn up?" Guido gasped.

"Of course she was. And it's all your fault. 'Cause of you, she went and shouldered the whole thing herself. She didn't tell the youngsters a thing. Now she's over in the States plotting God knows what."

That was valuable intel.

From what Gerde had said, they could infer that Soot, Scapulimancer, Flamefanner, and Bonfire had no idea about the Nostalgia Project. Hearth had intentionally kept them in the dark.

She was trying to bear the Nostalgia Project's burden all on her own.

"And you know what, sonny, I get how you feel. If I were a bit younger, I might be right there by your side trying to talk the boss down."

"........"

Guido clutched his sword's handle tight.

"Once age got the better of me, I started teaching my techniques to as many kids as I could. Heide and those idiot twins ran away from my training, but Little Klaus and plenty of other people inherited my skills."

"............."

"My knowledge and techniques will outlive me. That's plenty. For me, that's plenty..." Gerde sucked in a deep breath, then bellowed right at Guido. "So pull yourself together and quit your blubbering already!! You're a grown-ass man, for crying out loud!!"

Guido drew his sword from its sheath.

White Spider was only able to see it for the briefest of moments. However, the way it gleamed was something he would never forget.

A beat later, blood exploded from Gerde's body, and she perished with a faint smile on her lips.

That was the true cause of Inferno's destruction—an internal schism.

Serpent had helped bring it about, to be sure, but it was something they never could have achieved on their own. If White Spider had simply kept making moves at random, then some intelligence agency or another would eventually have crushed them. Without Guido's strong conviction, they never would have achieved the successes they did.

The Nostalgia Project was the ultimate sin, and the different approaches to that sin tore the greatest spy team in the world apart.

"Hearth" Veronika chose to shoulder all that sin herself and bring the Project to fruition.

"Torchlight" Guido chose to stop the sin and stand against her.

Both of them sacrificed themselves for the sake of what they believed in. The rest of the team's deaths were simply collateral damage, nothing more.

An era was at its end.

◇◇◇

The moment Guido struck Firewalker down, there was something inside White Spider that told him the mission was complete. Sure enough, successful reports came in one after another. Purple Ant took care of Hearth in the United States of Mouzaia; Indigo Grasshopper took care of Soot and Scapulimancer in the Lylat Kingdom; and Black Mantis took care of Flamefanner in the Galgad Empire.

They sent all the bodies back to the Din Republic.

They did so out of respect for their status as legendary spies, and also because Guido had insisted that they do so. He wanted them to at least get to rest in the same grave.

White Spider breathed a sigh of relief. It had been a big mission, and it felt good to wrap it up. He felt like he'd done his job, and that Serpent had grown into a respectable organization.

Purple Ant had become a force to be reckoned with. He didn't just murder Hearth, but famous spies from across the globe, and his work plunged the world's intelligence agencies into chaos. There was also Blue Fly, who boasted arguably the greatest combat skills in the world. On top of that, there was Black Mantis, who could cause even more damage than Blue Fly in localized areas; Green Butterfly, whose CIM leadership position allowed her to manipulate its agents as she pleased; Indigo Grasshopper, whose full talents were yet unplumbed; and Silver Cicada, who was growing and improving by the day.

Together, they had the power to take on the world.

Holy shit, we might actually be able to stop the Nostalgia Project.

It was hard to blame him for getting excited.

However, destroying Inferno had created a huge problem.

Neither Hearth nor Torchlight had told anyone about the situation they'd been faced with. After all, being a spy required both resolve and an ability to keep secrets.

That confluence of circumstances gave birth to a monster.

A monster who'd been left all alone, who'd been told nothing, and whose heart had just been lit with the flames of revenge.

◇◇◇

White Spider had been told about him, of course. He was Inferno's youngest member, the one who got stuck with all the grunt work. The global intelligence community had been taking notice of him as of late. Rumor had it that he'd inherited all of Inferno's skills and was going to be a major player in the coming generation.

"He's my pupil, so his skills are the real deal. He might have more raw talent than anyone else on the team," Guido told White Spider just before the attack on Inferno. However, Guido's appraisal wasn't all glowing. "But he's still a wet-behind-the-ears kid. His emotions are a big weakness of his. When push comes to shove, he always turns to his Inferno teammates. If you mess with his head, it'll knock off half his talent right then and there."

"I see, I see," Silver Cicada said as she listened from White Spider's side and jotted on her notepad. Once she'd figured out what trap she was going to lay for him, she immediately got to work making preparations.

All of a sudden, a thought crossed White Spider's mind. "You sure about this? Listening to you talk, it sounds like Bonfire's pretty taken with you."

"Sure he is. I raised him like a son."

"Couldn't we just win him over? I'd be happy to take a crack at it."

White Spider had no particular sympathy for Bonfire, he just figured that it was better not to let a potential asset go to waste. If the guy really had inherited techniques from all of Inferno, then that made him plenty monstrous as far as White Spider was concerned.

"Not a chance." Guido shook his head. "I told you, my idiot pupil's too dependent on Inferno. He won't turn traitor. If we let a single Inferno member slip through our fingers, then they'll eventually follow in the boss's footsteps and become a threat to Serpent."

White Spider could hear a hint of sadness in Guido's voice. He must really have loved Bonfire in his own peculiar way. It did make sense—Guido was the one who originally found him. He'd raised Bonfire up, taken him on globe-trotting missions, and treated him to the local delicacies whenever they finished a job.

As White Spider was reflecting on how insensitive his question had been, Guido continued. "But y'know," he murmured, "if by some impossible stroke of fate, he manages to overcome this, if he finally figures out how to fight on his own..."

The corners of his mouth curled ever-so-slightly upward.

"Then when that happens, that idiot pupil of mine…he really might become the Greatest Spy in the World."

There was too much self-deprecation in Guido's expression to call it hope, yet too much of a smile to call it concern. White Spider wondered if Guido knew how conflicted he looked. He very nearly asked, but he decided not to. Perhaps that half-assed nature of his was his weakness. White Spider was surprised that a man like Guido had such a flaw.

One way or the other, though, White Spider didn't really take any of what Guido was saying seriously.

Thinking back now, that was probably the point where the wheels started coming off.

Silver Cicada got struck down.

When White Spider heard the news, he was shocked. *She seriously lost?* At that point, though, he wasn't too concerned yet. Guido had offered to eliminate Bonfire himself. Inferno had officially been on a mission to retrieve the Abyss Doll bioweapon, and Guido was going to take advantage of that to set a trap.

With him on the job, White Spider was sure they had nothing to worry about.

Then Guido lost, too.

White Spider saw it happen himself, and he could barely believe his own eyes. Someone must have screwed up. Considering the way Guido took the bullet White Spider had meant for Klaus, maybe he'd been going easy on him in the fight, too.

Next time, though, White Spider was going to kill Bonfire for sure. After all, he knew every last thing about the man. Bonfire was far stronger than him, but that didn't mean he was unbeatable. The fact that White Spider managed to escape their confrontation in the Din Republic entertainment district was evidence of that.

Purple Ant, Black Mantis, or Indigo Grasshopper—surely any one of them could take him down.

Then Purple Ant lost and got captured.

In the blink of an eye, Serpent had lost three members. Not just that, but White Spider had really relied on Purple Ant and Blue Fly. The two of them had been Serpent's wings, and yet a single man had just hewn them both off.

All of Guido's fears had come to pass—"Bonfire" Klaus had become the Greatest Spy in the World.

A tsunami of terror surged over White Spider and swallowed him whole.

He needed to kill Bonfire immediately.

That much was obvious, but what he couldn't figure out was *how.* Not even Purple Ant had been able to take him down. If White rallied his team without a plan, they were liable to get beaten, too. His trusty Blue Fly was gone now.

On the night Purple Ant got captured, White Spider sat in his smuggler's ship cabin and groaned. The radio conversation he'd had with Bonfire back in the city of Mitario still lingered in his ears.

"I see he wasn't working alone. How about that rematch, then?"

It had taken everything White Spider had to hide how badly he was shaking. Fighting Bonfire wasn't an option. White Spider could never hope to match a man like that.

"Dammit, Guido. You were right," he muttered, his voice barely coherent. "I didn't have enough conviction. Hell, I didn't even understand what I was getting myself into, not really. I didn't get what you meant when you said we were making enemies of the status quo itself..."

He punched the wall so hard his hand bled.

"Ugh... He really is such a pain in Serpent's ass. I'm gonna kill him. I seriously am. I'm done with this brute-force nonsense. I gotta look at every angle, work through all the details, and come up with a plan that'll put him down for good," he said, echoing his words from back in Mitario. "If the weak are meat and the strong do eat…then that guy's eating good."

It had taken White Spider years to gather his team, and Bonfire was tearing through them like they were nothing. Even now, he was probably hard at work trying to track White Spider down. Only now did White Spider realize how merciful it had been of Guido to spare his life just for sobbing and begging. He doubted that Serpent's boss or Indigo Grasshopper would have any idea how to deal with Bonfire, either.

Bonfire was the man who would eventually pick up "Hearth" Veronika's torch and destroy Serpent. Then he would carry out the Nostalgia Project, killing countless millions of the weak and leaving a world where only the strong got to thrive.

Beating him with raw power was a nonstarter. Blue Fly and Purple Ant had proved as much.

"You know what, I gotta get dirtier. If I wanna overturn the status quo, I gotta become the cowardliest, sneakiest, nastiest son of a bitch the world has ever seen."

That marked the day where White Spider started gradually warping his personality.

He needed to be Klaus's opposite—to reach the deepest nadir of weakness.

"Look, it's not my faaaault!!"

It was four months after Purple Ant's capture, and White Spider was getting plastered in the city of Hurough.

Today was a momentous day, and in his excitement, he'd rented out an entire hotel suite. It was an extravagant expense, and one that was going to have serious repercussions for his cashflow, but he decided that that could be a problem for tomorrow.

As he drank his favorite beer straight from the bottle, he gazed out at the Hurough cityscape down below. To him, all it looked like was the nation that had bombed his hometown to the ground.

"The thing about weaklings like me is, we gotta play dirty if we ever wanna win! It just is what it is. So sure, maybe I'm a bit underhanded, but it's 'cause I'm weak. But then everyone goes and holds it against me while the strong fucks get to strut around in public while everyone loves 'em! It's not faaaaaaaaaaaaaaaair!"

He hurled his beer bottle against the wall, then turned his gaze to the girl.

"You get where I'm coming from, don't you, 'Glide' Qulle?"

There was a girl standing in the corner of the room. Her expression was mournful, and there were tears rolling down her cheeks.

She was a member of a Din Republic spy team called Avian. Her jade-green hair was tied back in a ponytail, and she was wearing glasses. Her eyes normally held more dignity than this, but at the moment, there were fat tears pooling in their corners.

Green Butterfly was working as a member of the CIM's leadership, and she was the one who'd tipped White Spider off about a Din team trying to dig up information on Firewalker. That had caught White Spider's interest. If a Din spy got killed or went missing, there was a good chance it would be Lamplight who inherited their mission. Working together with Green Butterfly, White Spider laid a trap for one of the Din team's members.

"If I give you information about Lamplight," Qulle said, her shoulders trembling in humiliation, "you'll really let Avian live?"

"Yeah, absolutely. I can be a generous man when people turn traitor for me."

As it turned out, that was White Spider's lucky day. Avian actually knew Lamplight's members. It was such a fortuitous coincidence he nearly let out a cry of joy. White Spider had come across plenty of Din spies, but not a single one of them had any solid intel on Lamplight.

"Of course, all of that is predicated on your information being true. It wasn't up close, but I've seen those Lamplight kids before. If you try to feed me any bullshit, I'll know."

"………"

"Also, I am gonna have to keep Avian locked up for a bit."

Avian going missing would summon Bonfire just as well as them dying, so it was all about the same to White Spider.

Qulle bit down hard on her lip, then handed him an envelope.

White Spider quickly flipped through its contents. Inside, there was a list of every Lamplight member's appearance and verbal tics. White Spider had seen Lamplight twice. It had been through a scope, so he hadn't picked up on many details, but Qulle's report seemed to check out.

"Nice, you pass. Avian can live."

"I really appreciate it. It's just…" Qulle hesitated for a moment. "There's one more piece of secret Lamplight intel, one that I didn't write in there."

"Huh?"

"If you'd lend me your ear for a second…"

She lowered her voice and slowly walked over to White Spider.

When she got close, she cupped her hand around her mouth and brought her face right up to his ear.

"………Go fuck yourself."

She whipped a knife out of her sleeve and lashed out with it.

White Spider didn't panic. After dodging the thrust aimed at his throat, he kicked Qulle into the air and grabbed the pistol he'd left lying nearby. "Yeah, I figured that was where this was headed."

"Rgh!"

"You needed a better plan. I gotta say, there's no one I hate more than people who can't decide if they're weak or strong. If you beg for your life, I'd be willing to hear you out."

Qulle bit down hard on her lip. "We're not going to lose to you!"

She hurled her knife at him and, in the same breath, turned and fled the suite.

White Spider didn't bother chasing her. After all, he already knew where she was going.

He picked up the phone and called Green Butterfly using a special direct CIM line. "Change of plans. Qulle tried to screw us."

There was something strangely exciting about saying it aloud.

* * *

"I want everyone on Avian dead."

White Spider was glad all over again that he'd chosen to celebrate. Today was the day he took the fight straight to Bonfire, and that was something worth commemorating.

Attacking Bonfire head-on was a fool's errand.

White Spider knew that, so he laid a trap to ensnare Lamplight.

By having Belias kill Avian, he could get Belias and Lamplight to fight. Then he could get someone on Lamplight to turn traitor and have them fight their boss Bonfire to the death.

Using the intel Qulle gave him, he surveilled Lamplight when they came to the Commonwealth and figured out that Monika was in love. Once he did, he took advantage of Prince Darryn's assassination to get her to betray her team.

In a perfect world, he would have liked the CIM and Lamplight to get into an all-out war, but Monika put a stop to that.

Little by little, though, his wish was coming true. Now he was just one step away from being able to kill the Greatest Spy in the World.

By the time White Spider finished the novel, the sun had long since risen.

Without so much as skimming back over the manuscript, he popped it straight in an envelope. "This baby here's gonna be a bestseller for sure. I never knew I had such a knack for writing. Looks like the world just found its newest literary genius."

White Spider knew better than to include any details that could be traced back to Serpent, and he made sure to throw plenty of lies in with the truth. Then, for the big finale, he killed all the characters off in a massive explosion.

"All right, guess I'd better get to work now."

White Spider headed out into the city.

He had plans to pick up some confidential intel from a CIM mole. Taking care not to get followed, he retrieved a note from beneath a park bench. It listed out the location for the meet—an abandoned clinic. After making sure it wasn't a trap, White Spider headed in.

White Spider's CIM informant was waiting for him inside. The man handed him a sheet of paper. "Read it quick, then destroy it."

On the paper, he'd listed out the CIM's guard formation for the royal funeral.

White Spider didn't need to be told twice. He skimmed through the intel at record speed.

Yeah, that's pretty much what I expected. Most of the security is gonna be police and military. Those guys won't be a problem. It's the CIM agents working behind the scenes I gotta worry about.

The report also contained the location of the room where Klaus was being held. Getting there would be a challenge. There were loads of guards, and even if White Spider made it there, every minute the assassination took to carry out increased the odds he'd get spotted.

Now, how're we gonna skin this cat...?

As his thoughts began turning, his gaze landed on the document's final section.

At the moment, there's a false rumor going through the CIM. It alleges...

The way it had been bolded gave White Spider a nasty premonition. He read the passage through to its end.

...that the Avian spies are still alive.

"Keeping things interesting, are we?"

Lamplight were the ones who'd planted the rumor, he was sure of it. They were the only ones who would ever devise a plan that absurd. He had no idea what they hoped to achieve, but they were clearly up to something.

However, White Spider had no problem with that. They were spies, and from here on out, everyone was going to be piling lie on top of lie on top of lie in an attempt to finesse each other and get the upper hand.

"Come on, I gave you the intel you asked for," the informant snapped at him. "Now it's your turn to talk. You said you knew, right? You said you'd tell me who really killed Prince Darryn—"

"Yeah, of course I do. You're looking at him. And now *I'm through with you.*"

White Spider pulled out his concealed pistol and shot the man right through the head.

"Look, man, I really do try to be generous when people turn traitor for me. But at the end of the day, I'm kind of a piece of shit. Sometimes, I don't exactly keep all my promises."

He clasped his hands together in prayer for the corpse he'd just made, then left the clinic.

"And sometimes, sacrifices have to be made. We all gotta pitch in to protect the world from the ultimate sin—and you're up next, Bonfire."

That was who White Spider—the man who essentially built Serpent from the ground up—really was.

He'd been instrumental in manifesting the pipe dream Serpent's boss and Indigo Grasshopper had laid out, and he'd grown into a spy who could rival all the intelligence agencies of the world. None of that would have been possible without his talents.

There was something that man knew in his bones—that if he didn't stop Klaus, then Serpent was done for.

The final battle, the one that Serpent and Inferno's survivors were staking everything on, was about to begin.

Chapter 3
Resurrection

In an apartment off in a remote corner of the city, a pair of agents were frowning at something.

The many massive factories that had sprouted up during the industrial revolution two centuries prior had been both a boon and a bane for the city of Hurough. The military might they afforded the nation allowed them to place much of the world under colonial rule, but at the same time, the factories' filthy soot choked the city, inflicting pneumonia on the local workers and driving them to poverty.

The spies were investigating a strip where those so afflicted tended to gather. Crime and prostitution were rampant in the area, and it had once given birth to a homicidal Ripper. The apartment complexes there were a haven for people with shady pasts, and the spies barged into one building after another.

"Looks like this one's empty, too."

"Are you sure it wasn't just bullshit? Those Din spies could've just been making it all up."

The two men made no efforts to hide their displeasure.

"Those Avian guys are dead. There's no way they're still alive."

The two spies worked for the CIM as members of Vanajin squad four, the one led by "Swordsmith" Miné. Last night, their boss had given them a sudden order: Track down the spy team known as Avian.

However, their hearts weren't really in it.

"Yeah, I'm with you there. I get that this was an order straight from the boss, but why send us on this goose chase when our plates are full enough as it is?"

"'Cause they might have intel on Serpent, that's why."

"You really believe that?"

"Belias attacked them but couldn't finish them off. Word is, Avian and Serpent got into a fight just afterward. That means they might have information we could use."

After checking to make sure they were alone, the two men began discussing the matter openly.

"And plus, something weird just happened. Someone snuck into a Vanajin base yesterday."

"Wait, seriously?"

"We don't have any proof it was Avian that did it, but the secret message we found in the office implies it was a Din spy. It's like they wanted us to know they were there."

"...Couldn't it just have been someone from Lamplight?"

"Nah, the CIM's got them all under heavy surveillance. And that includes the Avian survivor Cloud Drift, too." After pointing out that there was obviously a chance it was some other Din spy, the man went on. "The way I see it, there's a nonzero chance that Avian's members are still alive and kicking."

An ominous chill came over them, and they grimaced and left the apartment.

What they didn't know was, *someone had been watching them that whole time.*

That someone was Lamplight's newest spy—code name Insight.

Insight had been hiding on the roof and keeping tabs on the men. Neither of them even noticed Insight was there. When it came to masking their presence, Insight was profoundly confident in their own skills.

From what Insight could tell, the girls were making their move.

After observing the two men, Insight started working out a plan as well. They were going to have to be smart about this. They owed Lamplight a great debt, and they were determined to repay it.

The CIM had lent Sara, Sybilla, and Lily a room in their main office, and the girls had access to three meals a day and beds they could sleep in, and if they asked, they could even take showers. They were being watched twenty-four seven, but aside from that, their living conditions were more than fair.

That said, they were under a number of restrictions.

For one, they weren't allowed to see Klaus. He was under especially tight surveillance. The girls had deduced that he was in a building nearby, but the CIM wouldn't even let them get close to it.

For another, Miné never let them out of her sight.

"Ah-ha-ha, would you please stop spreading those obnoxious rumors? I mean, come on. Avian being alive?! You're really getting on my nerves!" she cackled from inside their assigned room.

"It's no rumor. It's true," Sybilla said as she cleaned her pistol. She shot Miné a glare. "Avian survived. Belias couldn't kill 'em, and neither could Serpent. Hurry up and track 'em down already, wouldja? We need to touch base."

That was the rumor the girls had been working so hard to spread. They'd been telling every CIM agent they came across, not just Miné, that the corpses had been fakes. After making themselves look like they were dead, Avian had gone underground. Lamplight had only seen photos of the bodies, so they hadn't realized they were fakes at the time, but a few days ago, Lamplight had found a coded message from them that only Lamplight was able to decode.

Amelie came by at one point, and when they told her, a brief look of surprise had crossed her face. "...If that's true, then those are glad tidings indeed," she murmured, then began arranging for her colleagues to begin searching for them.

Now Miné frowned in annoyance. "Actually, the search is ending today."

"The hell?"

"I put a stop to it. We can't afford to waste any more man-hours on your nonsense. They're dead. End of story." After letting out another of her trademark laughs, she narrowed her eyes at them. "Unless, what, was this all part of some secret plan of yours?"

Sybilla clicked her tongue and glared right back. "Maybe it was, maybe it wasn't. Figure it out yourself."

Realizing how tense the mood was, Lily came rushing over from the other side of the room. "Now, now, you two. Remember, we're all friends here." She brought with her a tray laden with teacups. "How about we all have some tea? I bought up loads and loads of high-end leaves."

There were four cups in all.

"This'll help you keep your mind off things," Lily said as she set the tray in front of Miné. "And plus, it's so tasty I got carried away and brewed way too much, so you'd basically be doing me a favor. Besides, if I run out, I can always ask our good buddies in the CIM to go out and buy us more."

"If anyone's picking a fight here, it's you!" Miné howled.

There were two large teapots sitting behind Lily's back.

Miné squeezed the bridge of her nose. "I've never seen anything like it," she grumbled. "What kind of detainee has the *audacity* to send her own wardens out to buy tea cakes and cosmetics for her?"

"What? But Miné, it seemed like you didn't want us going outside, so—"

"That doesn't mean you can just use my people as your errand boys!"

As the two of them butted heads, Sara let out a weak laugh from beside them. "Ha-ha…"

The four of them were sitting around the table in the middle of the room. It was time for a strategy meeting. They would've liked to kick Miné out, but sadly that wasn't an option.

"Here's the situation as it stands," Lily said to get the ball rolling. "Right now, we have exactly one mission—capturing that jerk-face White Spider."

Sybilla and Sara nodded in agreement. At that point, it hardly bore repeating. They needed to apprehend White Spider so they could press him for information on Monika's whereabouts.

"We're betting that White Spider wants to come assassinate Teach.

The odds he'll try are pretty good, and when he does, we know that he's probably going to do it—"

"—by getting someone in the CIM to turn traitor."

After finishing Lily's sentence, Sara gulped. That was something Grete had pointed out to them—the possibility of a new traitor.

"Ah-ha-ha, that could never happen! The CIM's unity will never waver!" Miné laughed from across the table as she sipped her tea, but the girls ignored her. She was free to believe what she wanted.

Sybilla crossed her arms on the table. "As long as they're keepin' the boss locked up, it'd be pretty hard to whack him without havin' someone on the inside. Even with the CIM's forces spread thin, there's no way he could just punch his way through."

"Yeah," Lily replied. "In other words, we need to root out the mole."

"What's Grete got to say about that?"

"Grete's smart, but not even she can pin down the traitor while she's cooped up in the hospital. Still, she did give us a guess. The traitor needs to be someone who can meddle with the CIM's guard assignments."

No matter how many bottom-level agents White Spider flipped, all it would do was cause a little bit of chaos. No, what they needed to be worried about were people with meaningful amounts of authority.

"In other words…one of the CIM's officers."

Once they'd finished summing up the situation, the girls let out long exhales. Lily twirled her hair around her finger with a strained expression, Sybilla covered her face with her hand, and Sara gave the puppy on her lap a big hug.

The three of them were stressed, and they had good reason to be. Prince Darryn's funeral was tomorrow. The day of reckoning had arrived all too fast, and tonight was the night that Klaus's guard assignment was going to be reduced. Foreign VIPs were streaming into the nation, and the CIM spies needed to shadow them to protect them from terrorism and assassination attempts.

If White Spider was going to come after Klaus, then his window was from tonight to the morning after next. If he missed it, it would give Klaus's leg a chance to heal, cost White Spider his once-in-a-lifetime opening, and leave Lamplight with no way of finding Monika. There was a huge amount riding on this for all parties involved.

"All right, let's make this count." Sybilla drummed on her knees, then rose to her feet. "It's time for that final officer meeting. Let's sniff out the traitor and tie 'em up!"

The CIM desperately wanted to capture the Serpent member responsible for Prince Darryn's death. They were holding a meeting to that effect, and they'd invited the girls.

"Yeah!" "Let's do this!" Lily and Sara cheered as they stood up as well.

"Ah-ha-ha!"

When they did, they were greeted by a grating peal of laughter.

Miné clutched at her chest and kicked her legs back and forth in a bemused display of mockery.

"The hell's your problem?" Sybilla asked. "We're free to suspect whoever we damn well please."

"No, no. I was supposed to keep it a secret until the very end, but I just can't hold it in anymore."

Miné's voice turned chilly.

"You people are the stupidest optimists I've ever seen."

The girls looked at her in confusion.

Rather than explain herself, Miné simply said, "The meeting's this way," and strode out of the room with the girls behind her.

There were six people sitting around the round table in the middle of the conference room.

The room had been built with a good distance between the walls and the table, no doubt to protect against listening devices. From what the girls had heard, the head of the Din Republic's Foreign Intelligence Office used a similar setup. That said, they doubted that room had a massive portrait of Her Majesty the Queen hanging on the wall the way the Fend Commonwealth's did.

When Miné led the girls into the room, the six CIM officers gave them a series of unfriendly looks.

Klaus and Amelie had already briefed them on who would be present.

There was "Puppeteer" Amelie, head of the special forces that answered directly to Hide.

There was "Armorer" Meredith, head of the agency's largest counterintelligence unit.

There was "Silhouette" Luke, head of the special assassination unit.

There was "Tracker" Sylvette, who also served as a lieutenant general in the Fend army.

There was "Jester" Heine, head of the engineering division.

And there was "Tunekeeper" Khaki, head of the unit in charge of manipulating the public.

These were elite spies, the kind of people that the girls usually wouldn't get to be in the same room as. They were the ones taking point on the current mission, and by the looks of it, they'd already gotten a head start.

Amelie was the one presiding over the meeting, and she quietly turned her gaze the girls' way. "Our guests from the Din Republic have experience combating Serpent. I called them here because I presumed you might have some questions they could help answer."

The officers' stares intensified.

The air in the conference room was so still you could hear a pin drop. The girls nearly forgot how to breathe.

However, they couldn't afford to be overpowered.

Someone in that room could very well be a traitor. This was their chance to figure out who that might be, and the people there were also their allies in the hunt for White Spider. This was no time to be losing their nerve.

Amelie had set the stage for them, and Lily stepped forward as the group's representative. "Um, hello. I'm Flower Garden from the Foreign Intelligence Office. If there's anything we can do to help capture White Spider, we're more than happy to—"

She trailed off midsentence.

The expressions of the six people around the table were stony. From the way they were looking at her, it wasn't even that they didn't trust her, but rather that they never had any interest in what she had to say in the first place.

"Huh?"

When Lily tilted her head in confusion, one of the six spoke up. "Enough of this already, Amelie."

The speaker was a man with dark skin and a mass of blond hair resembling a lion's mane. Lily recognized him—that was "Armorer" Meredith, the man who'd apprehended them and Miné's superior officer.

"Bonfire would have been one thing, but these people have nothing to offer us. I have no interest in playing along with this farce."

"I'm sorry, what?"

"Miné, do it."

Rather than answer Lily's question, Miné let out a big laugh. "Ah-ha-ha, I'm on it," she said as she strode on over to them.

She held out her hands and gave them a small, smug head tilt.

"Hand over every weapon you've got."

They hoped they'd misheard her. However, the mood in the room didn't lighten in the slightest. Miné repeated herself, more forcefully this time. "Your weapons, now. Until the funeral's over, you're not allowed to have any arms whatsoever."

"Hold on! Wh-what're you talkin' about?!" Sybilla cried out in surprise. She slipped past Miné and addressed the officers. "What the hell?! We wanna capture White Spider just as bad as—"

"Just two days ago, one of my little agents was killed. He was found in a local clinic." The speaker was Tunekeeper, a monocled man wearing a white gown. "There are eyewitness accounts suggesting that he met with a Din Republic spy just before his death. You can hardly blame us for distrusting you."

"Oh, fuck off. You've been watchin' us this whole—"

"You're the ones who've been suggesting that Avian is still alive, aren't you? We don't know if it's true or not, but it's certainly cause for suspicion."

The other officers agreed with him. Silhouette, an odd-looking man with an animal mask over his face, gave him a silent nod, and Jester, a slightly plump woman wearing a vividly purple dress, shot the girls a look of contempt.

Sybilla tried to get up in their faces, but Miné grabbed her by the back of her head and slammed her into the round table. "Ah-ha-ha, quit resisting!"

Lily and Sara rushed over to pull her off, but Meredith stopped them with a glare.

"You have only yourselves to blame. This is what you get for spreading those rumors," Miné said, still keeping her grip on Sybilla's head. "Screw you for making us play along with your dumb lies. Avian is dead and buried! You're never going to see them again!"

Sybilla bit down on her lip. "......!"

"And anyway, we were never planning on turning to *you* people for help." Miné yanked on Sybilla's hair to forcefully lift her head. "If you've got any problems with that, then we can throw down right here. You lot against us."

".........!!"

The officers' stares made it clear that this wasn't a request.

The girls had no choice. There was no way they could take on all those Fend Commonwealth elites.

Miné delivered the finisher with a pleased laugh. "Then in that case, you backwater handmaids can go back to your room and twiddle your thumbs."

After getting cast from the room like so much garbage, the girls got carted back to their assigned room.

"Bye now. *I* actually have work to do," Miné cackled, then left again. There was a hint of sweat beading on her face, but the girls had no idea why that might be.

The CIM had confiscated all of their weapons. They'd taken the girls' knives, pistols, steel wire, and even the needles they kept hidden in their sleeves and collars. Between those and the poison gas emitter they'd taken from its hiding spot beneath Lily's ample bosom, the girls had been completely cleaned out.

The entire procedure had taken place in the conference room—that was to say, right in front of all the head officers. It was humiliating, like the CIM wanted to remind them who held the power here. If anything, that stung more than the disarming itself.

"Damn, they beat us to the punch."

"Yeah…"

Sara glumly sat down in her chair and petted her puppy. At least they'd had the decency not to take her dog. Either that, or they just didn't want to have to look after him.

Odds are, White Spider was the one behind that murder. We don't know shit about that. Sybilla gave her tongue a loud click. *I can't believe they're keepin' us from puttin' up a decent fight…*

They and the CIM may have been allies, but by no means did that mean they were friends. Everything that had just happened made that obvious, if it wasn't already. At no point had the CIM actually been planning on accepting their help. If anything, the fact that they were even moving around freely was a pain in the CIM's neck. The only thing the CIM wanted from them was to sit still in their room and shut up.

The girls were in no position to root out the traitor.

The sun began setting, and the light streaming in through the window grew weaker. Chances were, it wouldn't be long before White Spider started trying to murder Klaus. As a matter of fact, he might be making a move at that very moment.

"Okay, what's the play?" Lily's voice was uncharacteristically calm. She spun her pot of black tea around in her hands, not looking dejected in the slightest. "For the record, leaving this up to the CIM might be a better idea than it sounds."

"Sorry, run that by me again?"

"The CIM is full of talented spies, right? They might just go and capture White Spider without us having to lift a finger. Heck, we could just take a nap. It doesn't get any easier than that." She smirked. "And most importantly, Teach isn't just gonna take this lying down. I'm sure he has some sort of plan. Instead of butting in and making a mess of things, the smart thing for us to do might just be nothing."

"………"

There was certainly a logic to what Lily was saying. The CIM had no desire to let White Spider escape. They viewed Monika as the killer and White Spider as one of her co-conspirators. Even stretched thin as they were, that was one thing they weren't going to cut corners on.

However, Sybilla's fists were trembling.

"Annette's tryin' to change."

"Huh?"

"You saw her back at the hospital. Even that little menace is tryin' to face forward."

The image in Sybilla's mind was of that ash-pink-haired girl, and of the happy smile she'd given them.

It happened two days prior—that was, the day after they returned Annette to the hospital from her escape attempt.

Annette was back in her hospital room, and she'd regained her composure. She'd gotten away with only a minor aggravation of her wounds, and she was certainly well enough to stuff her cheeks full of the sweets the others brought her.

Now that they'd glimpsed Annette's dark side, Lily and Sybilla came in a little nervous. However, they couldn't help but loosen up when they saw Sara doting on Annette just like always. "Say 'aah,' Miss Annette," Sara said as she fed Annette some milk pudding, to which Annette replied, "I love ya, Sis!"

At the end of the day, Annette was still Annette. This was just another of their adorable problem child's many eccentricities. That was all there was to it.

That said, there had been one big change. Annette no longer made any efforts to hide her bloodlust.

"By the way, I'm still planning on murdering Monika!"

""You're incorrigible!!"" Lily and Sybilla roared at the hospital room confession.

Annette let out a cackle. "She hurt my toy Erna and called me a runt. She's dead to me, yo."

"Your, uh, your toy?"

"But the thing is, I'm not strong enough to beat her right now..." She stuck out her tongue a little. "...so I guess I have to find a new way to kill people."

She beamed as though she'd just had a huge burden lifted off her.

Annette was starting to come off less as a rascal and more as an out-and-out villain, but the others decided to view it in a positive light.

This was the first time they'd seen Annette try to improve herself, and they wanted to support her on her journey.

As she thought back to Annette's transformation, Sybilla sucked in another breath. "Seein' her smile like that made me realize somethin'. I gotta change, too."

"Huh? Why's that?" Lily asked, scrunching up her lips in confusion.

"I couldn't save Monika." Sybilla poured her strength into every word. "She put everything on her own back, and I wasn't able to do shit for her. I know she rejected the boss's help and decided to fight the CIM solo, but still."

Sybilla realized now just how stupid the things she said back then were.

"What the fuck have you even been doing?!"

Of all the people, she'd chosen to direct her anger at Klaus. When she learned that they'd failed to stop Monika from leaving Lamplight, her frustration had gotten the better of her.

"There was this part of me that believed… I figured that in spite of everything, that you'd find some way to fix it…"

She'd pretended not to notice her own shortcomings and lashed out like a child. If anyone needed to grow up, it was her.

"I'm doin' this! Like hell I'm gonna sit here and pass all my work off to others." She slammed the table and rose to her feet. "I'm not gonna let people take jack from me anymore! Not the boss, not Monika, not nothin'!"

"I'm loving this enthusiasm, but do you have any evidence that we need to make a move? Enough evidence it's worth turning the CIM against us?"

"Our situation's all the proof I need. White Spider told his mole to steal our weapons. He's scared we're gonna ruin his plan just like Monika did his last one!"

Sybilla might have been reading too much into things, but that didn't seem likely. She was right—it didn't make any sense for the CIM to confiscate their weapons when they did.

"The traitor's already gettin' to work—so we gotta save the boss, stat!"

* * *

If the traitor was already trying to kill Klaus, then the whole thing could be over before they knew it.

"You're right! I feel bad for the CIM, but we can't afford to trust them!" Sara said, rising to her feet as well. "We need to figure this out. I promised myself I would become a spy who could protect everyone!"

"Looks like your girl Wunderkind Lily's the one who's got her head on straightest right now, so lemme remind you of something." Lily continued twirling her teapot. Her eyes were cold and rational. "Worst case scenario, this could end in us having to fight the CIM again. We were able to make an alliance with them thanks to Monika, and this would send us right back to square one."

""We're still doing it.""

"I guess there's no talking you out of this, huh?" Lily followed their lead and stood up. She gave them a bemused shrug, then grinned like that was what she'd been expecting all along. "Well, I've already finished all my prep. I brewed up plenty of tea."

She went over to the table and picked up the other teapot. Each pot was full to the brim, and she held one up in each hand and swished them around.

"Oh, hey, thanks," Sybilla said cheerfully. "Then once we've had some to psych ourselves up—"

"I wouldn't do that if I were you. It's poisoned."

"What?"

"I figured this might happen, so I moved all my poison and antidote over before they could steal it."

Lily stuck her index finger in one of the pots and pulled it out. Sinister-looking droplets glistened on her fingertip. Lily had mixed her poison in with the black tea. Meanwhile, the antidote capable of neutralizing it was over in the other teapot.

She licked up the poison on her fingertip and took a moment to savor it. "Now, let's do this. We're gonna lay a trap for those CIM numbnuts so good they won't know what hit them."

The girls wasted no time in getting ready. They transferred the poisoned tea and the antidote tea into perfume bottles. Then they smashed

the porcelain teapots and sharpened the shards into knives. Each one was only about the size of a thumb, but that was more than enough to slice through someone's carotid artery.

By the time they were finished, it was about ten at night.

They were entering the time frame where Grete had predicted that White Spider was likely to launch his attack.

The girls escaped the CIM office via the window. Using the window frame as a handhold, they climbed onto the roof, then ran across it and leaped over the fence surrounding the building.

"Where's the boss at?!" Sybilla shouted.

"He's in that building over there," Sara replied. "Once we get closer, I can track his exact position by smell."

The place she was pointing at was a multistory building a few hundred feet from the main CIM office. It was under CIM ownership, and it was the one place that the girls had been kept thoroughly away from.

Johnny the puppy let out a small bark and raced toward their destination. Once they got there, the plan was to have him follow Klaus's scent.

Naturally, though, that was going to be easier said than done.

There was someone running across the CIM roof just like the girls had, and they were closing in quick. They were faster than Lily and Sara, and before the girls knew what happened, their pursuer managed to cut in front of them.

"Stop right there!"

It was Miné. She was already holding her sonic weapon at the ready.

"Ah-ha-ha, what gives? The hell you think you're doing, strolling around without supervision—"

Sybilla stopped in her tracks and waved Miné off like a bug. "We're free to go wherever we goddamn please."

Miné was clearly anxious. She bit down on her lip. "........."

Upon seeing her expression, Sybilla broke into a triumphant grin. "If you people were gonna lock us up, you woulda just done it from the start. Awfully kind of you, lettin' us walk around freely as long as we took a babysitter along." She stuck out her tongue. "I bet our boss didn't give you a choice, did he?"

Lily was the one who'd figured it out. Their restrictions had been oddly lenient, and that meant that the CIM probably wasn't allowed to fully detain them.

"Stay out of our way. If you really gotta, you can follow along to keep an eye on us."

Big droplets of sweat began beading on Miné's forehead.

As Sybilla strode past her, she shot a meaningful look over to Lily. Before they went to see Klaus, there was one last piece of business they needed to attend to.

"What am I going to do with you lot?" Miné slumped her shoulders in exasperation. "Look, can you at least wait a minute? I can't just go running off at a moment's notice, I need to report in to my—"

The girls were having none of that.

Ignoring Miné's request, they took off at a dash through the city. The route they took wasn't the most direct path to the building Klaus was in. Instead, they headed in the direction with the least foot traffic.

Eventually, they made their way into a large abandoned building.

The building was completely empty. It was four stories tall and slated for demolition soon.

"Why here?" Miné asked with a confused tilt of the head, but she followed them inside nonetheless.

There was a large hall on the first floor. The floor still had traces of the restaurant it had once housed.

When the girls got to the center of the hall, they came to a stop.

"By the way," Lily said, "about Avian."

"What about them?" Miné asked in confusion.

"There were a whole bunch of reasons why we wanted you guys looking for them. One of those reasons is 'cause we figured that if someone was real dumb, we might flush them out." Lily spun around and gave Miné a big smile. "Tell me, how is it you were so sure they were dead?"

"What are you talking about? It was my own colleagues that put them—"

"You couldn't have been, not with the intel the CIM has."

Her eyes had a steely look in them, and they were focused squarely on Miné.

Sybilla and Sara slowly repositioned themselves until they were surrounding the CIM agent.

Lily continued her explanation. "Not even Amelie was there when Flock, Glide, Lander, and Feather were killed. She just assumed what happened from context."

She was right—the only one the CIM could be absolutely certain was dead was "South Wind" Queneau, who'd died protecting his teammates. Beyond that point, Amelie had no idea what exactly had gone down.

Miné's voice started growing increasingly frantic. "But she must have been able to identify them from the corpses—"

"Nah, no way. Belias had no idea why they were attacking Avian. They were just doing what Green Butterfly—that's a CIM traitor, by the way—told them to."

It was hard to imagine Amelie having had any detailed intelligence on Avian. She had just been following orders. That was why she'd misjudged their skill so badly, and that was how she'd gotten so many of her agents injured.

As further proof, Amelie didn't refute it when the girls told her that Avian was still alive. And the Tunekeeper man had been the same. He said that they didn't know if the reports of Avian's death were true or not.

"So the idea that Avian survived really wasn't all that absurd. It could've been true."

Lily raised her voice.

"Except to Serpent. *The only people who would've had their minds made up about Avian were the ones who actually killed them.*"

Miné had messed up.

When she called off the search, she should have just said the part about not having enough man-hours. She shouldn't have given Avian being dead as a reason.

After all, there wasn't a single person in the CIM that could say that with any certainty.

"Now, I'll be the first to admit," Lily said, "those are some big leaps of logic. There's a chance you're just confused, or that you put too much faith in Belias's report."

As Miné stood there frozen with her eyes wide open, Lily pointed a glass knife at her. Sara and Sybilla did the same with their porcelain counterparts.

"So I'm gonna need you to answer a simple question—are you planning on harming our teacher?"

A drop of sweat rolled down Miné's cheek and fell to the floor.

They heard a car drive by outside, but the sound soon died down. There weren't any residential buildings nearby, so the whole area cleared out quickly once night fell. The girls weren't interested in letting Miné call for help.

Miné sucked in a long, shallow breath. "Ah-ha-ha, why would I want to hurt Bonfire? Don't be silly."

Lily exchanged a look with Sybilla and Sara, then cracked her neck. "That's a lie."

"Huh?"

"*Pharma from Avian just told me.* She said you're lying."

"What?! What are you even talking about?!"

"Oh yeah, I forgot to mention. Avian came back from the dead."

"That doesn't make any sense! Now you're just making stuff up!" Miné roared. She couldn't help herself. The fake smile vanished from her face, and she pointed the sonic weapon in her hand straight at Lily. "If you keep pushing your luck, you'll leave me no choice but to fight back!" Her cries were downright shrill. "Know your place, handmaids! You're so quick to forget how helpless you were against my Absolute Reverb—"

"So sorry, but you're in checkmate," Lily spat. "You really gotta give us more credit."

"You were doomed from the moment you first drank my tea."

The sonic weapon tumbled from Miné's hand. Her fingers were twitching, and she couldn't muster any strength in them. "What did you do?"

"It's a slow-acting poison. It's probably getting pretty painful now, huh?"

Lily casually strolled over to her. When she gave Miné's shoulder a light push, Miné crumpled to her knees. Her expression was dumbfounded, and her face was drenched with sweat.

Now that Sybilla thought about it, Miné *had* been acting a little weird after the officers' meeting. She stole a look over at the smug expression on Lily's face.

Damn, she does not *fuck around.*

Lily slipped that poison into Miné's tea the moment Miné said that Avian was dead. At that point, their evidence against Miné was barely even circumstantial. What had Lily been planning on doing if her suspicions had been off the mark?

"Now, you'd best get talking." Lily pulled a vial of antidote out of her pocket and waved it in front of Miné's face. "Why were you planning on harming Teach? Whose orders are you acting on? If you don't talk fast, I can't promise you'll survive."

That part was a lie. The poison Lily was using only paralyzed the body for a couple of hours.

However, Miné had no way of knowing that. What she did know was that the poison was sapping her ability to move her own body, and the terror within her had to be mounting.

"And just for the record," Sybilla said for good measure, "I already nicked your radio. No one's comin' to save you."

She tossed the radio into the air and caught it to really drive the point home.

"Rrrrrrrrrrrrrrrrrrgh!" Miné's face went so red it was like it had just caught fire, and eventually, she shouted at the top of her lungs. "BOOOOOOOOOOSS! HEEEEEEEEEEELP!"

There was no way her SOS was going to reach anyone. The whole reason they'd lured her to the abandoned building was so that no one would hear her if she screamed. Still, they figured it would be best to shut her up, so they took a step toward her.

That was when a terrible rumble crashed over them like a flood.

By the time they realized that it was the rumble of footsteps, a massive figure came charging out of the shadows. The figure's charge was intense, and without any guns, the girls had no way of stopping them.

The attack their large foe had chosen was a shoulder tackle. Sybilla managed to step forward and intercept them at the very last moment, but not even she was able to fully counter the blow. She got sent tumbling, crashing into Lily and Sara behind her and taking them with her. Two of the perfume bottles Lily had been holding went rolling away.

"This is the antidote, is it? That was a brazen move." The massive figure was a man, and his voice was one the girls knew all too well. "I knew it would come to this. We should've just broken your legs back at the start."

There was a man who commanded the CIM's largest counterintelligence unit. A man with overwhelming strength, inexhaustible stamina, and ninety-six agents at his disposal. One of the CIM's head officers.

"All enemies of the Crown must hang."

Now, that very man—"Armorer" Meredith, Vanajin's boss—stood before them.

He popped open one of the antidote vials he'd taken from Lily and poured it down Miné's throat. "I'll be keeping the spare," he said as he tucked the other into his pocket.

The saber scabbard hanging at his waist glinted in the darkness. The girls could see fifteen more agents behind him, all of whom were glaring at them.

"You've gotta be kidding me," Lily groaned. "There's no way you should have been able to hear that scream…"

"What kind of boss fails to come running when one of his agents is in peril?" Meredith gave Miné an appreciative clap on the shoulder, then looked back at the girls. "More importantly, that was a rude thing you did back there. Why'd you poison my agent?"

"'Cause there's a chance she's in bed with Serpent," Sybilla replied bluntly. "As soon as we got our weapons confiscated, we knew you people had a mole. We can't trust you to protect the boss."

"So all you have is cheap slander." Meredith sighed and shook his head. In his eyes, they were nothing more than children throwing a tantrum. "Look, I'm not here to argue with you. We've got our own problems we're dealing with."

"And what're those?"

"I see no reason to tell you. If anyone's getting questioned here, it's the three people who just attacked my subordinate."

He reached for his saber's handle and strode toward them.

It would appear that talking things out wasn't an option. Meredith had every intention of attacking them. Was he the Serpent mole? Were he and his agent Miné plotting something together?

Either way, this was one fight they needed to avoid.

"Lily, Sara, run!"

As soon as Sybilla shouted, Lily grabbed Sara by the arm and took off at a dash. Dragging her bewildered teammate behind her, she made for the back exit.

The instant they did, Meredith let out a roar. "After them!! Don't let them escape!!"

"I just nicked this."

Sybilla took the hand grenade she'd stolen from Miné and tossed it toward Lily and Sara. The girls leaped out the exit, and the grenade brought the wall behind them crashing down.

The CIM agents running toward the back exit flinched, and Sybilla used that opening to circle over to the building's entrance. As far as she could tell, there were only two ways out of the building—the back entrance, and the front door. As long as she controlled the front door, Lily and Sara would be able to reach Klaus unopposed.

"I'm gonna need you all to stay put for a bit." She brandished the knife she'd taken off Miné. "You didn't want them gettin' away, but the feelin's mutual. Care to tell me about that problem you mentioned?"

The odds were stacked against her, but she didn't care.

Not only was she up against sixteen people, one of them was a CIM officer. Miné had once described Meredith as being a hundred times stronger than her, and Sybilla got the same vibes from him as she did other powerhouses like Klaus and Amelie. It didn't take a genius to see that she was outmatched.

In her head, though, she was thinking of the girl who'd squared off against several times more foes.

How much of a fight did Monika put up, I wonder?

Monika had risked her life to protect her team. If Sybilla wanted to call herself Lamplight's older sister, then backing down wasn't an option.

Looks like it's my turn to throw down the gauntlet!!

The time had come for her to put her life on the line, too.

Meredith scowled at her in annoyance. "You have no idea who you're messing with."

As soon as Sara and Lily escaped the building, an explosion sealed off the exit behind them.

Lily didn't even turn around. She just charged toward the building Klaus was in as fast as her legs would carry her.

"Miss Lily?!" Sara cried as the girl in question pulled her along. "Are you sure about this?! Is it really a good idea to leave Miss Sybilla alone with so many—"

With how many enemies there had been back there, Sara doubted that even Sybilla could emerge unscathed. Her prospects were grim.

"Of course it isn't!" Lily moaned in anguish. "Our plan was to just threaten Miné, then fool the rest of the CIM. As soon as we screwed that up, we lost. Seriously, how did that blond musclehead even do it? It's not fair!"

"Then—"

"But I'm still running!!"

Lily gave Sara's arm another tug.

They were a fair distance away from the abandoned building now. When Sara gave up on going back and focused on running, too, Lily let go of her arm.

"I know it's not the time, but as your leader, I need to give you a piece of my mind." Lily's voice was far harsher than normal. "The truth is, I think that goal of yours to become Lamplight's guardian is a pipe dream."

".........!"

"I mean, you're not exactly the first person I'd turn to in a pinch. Remember when we found out that Monika had betrayed us, and you weren't able to do a thing? You're not being realistic with yourself."

Sara had no rebuttal to that. Considering her skills, it was a fair assessment.

The night was silent save for the sound of their footsteps echoing on the pavement. At no point did Lily ever slow down.

"I get that that's the whole reason it's your goal. But if you really want to make that dream of yours come true, if you really have the guts to overturn the impossible…"

Her voice rang out crisp.

"…then the one thing you can never do is stop moving—*not even if you know you're going to lose.*"

Sybilla lasted all of four seconds.

She lay on the floor, collapsed on her hands and knees.

"Huh…?" she gasped in bewilderment.

She could taste the bitter flavor of dust filling her mouth. However, that was an afterthought compared to the terrible pain racking her body. The worst of it was in her spine, and it felt like her back and shoulders were broken. She doubted they actually were, but the blow she'd just taken was brutal enough that it sure could have fooled her. She could barely even breathe.

Wait, what the hell am I doin' on the floor?

She had yet to fully process the situation.

As she staggered to her feet, Meredith glared at her from up close.

What'd he do to me? What just happened?

She remembered taking her knife and charging at him with it. It was the one weapon she had. She'd stolen Miné's gun alongside it, but she'd already handed the gun off to Lily. She knew she needed to get in close before her opponent could open fire.

"What a pushover," Meredith had said.

The next moment, she'd hit the floor, landing back-first and then rolling from the sheer force of the blow. That was how she'd ended up on all fours. The pain in her body painted her a delayed picture of what had happened, but she still had no idea what exactly Meredith had done to her.

As Sybilla stared in confusion, Meredith stood before her with his saber at the ready.

"Did you think that if 'Flash Fire' Monika could do it, you could do it, too?"

The man had read her like a book.

"Your hubris knows no end." He sounded unimpressed. "The CIM runs intelligence for a nation with the greatest history of any in the world ruled by the mightiest of monarchs. You fail to comprehend the weight the title of officer in such an organization carries."

He swung his saber, and the air cracked in reply.

"All who face me fall, even Flash Fire. Make light of Armorer, guardian of the Crown, at your peril."

By the time Sybilla was back on her feet and readied her knife, Meredith was already on her.

"——!"

Blocking his saber blow sent her reeling.

"Even if you knew the trick, it wouldn't do you any good."

The saber's tip traced an arc through the air.

"I don't use my saber to stab or slice my foes. I use techniques that take advantage of its point."

Sure enough, Sybilla lost control of her center of gravity and collapsed back onto the ground.

Meredith was a force to be reckoned with.

The people of Hurough had mocked Vanajin as "violent" and "rowdy," but within the CIM itself, they were highly respected. And the efforts of "Armorer" Meredith formed the team's bedrock. The sight of him using his inhuman stamina to fight valiantly day and night was enough to move anyone. He was always the first into the fray when his nation was in danger, and anyone who hurt his subordinates would face his wrath. The esteem of his ninety-six agents drove them to compete with each other and achieve as much as they could. Puppeteer commanded her forces from the rearguard with exacting precision, but the charisma he possessed was of the exact opposite sort.

When faced with his stellar physique, even Monika had chosen to avoid fighting him head-on and focused instead on fleeing.

All that to say, *Sybilla was completely and utterly outmatched.*

If someone had walked in without knowing what was happening, it would have been hard to even look at the sight they found. What you had was a brawny, full-grown man delivering a brutal beatdown to an underage girl. Sybilla was doing a decent job using her knife to defend against his saber, but Meredith started using his saber for feints and throwing in kicks and punches. Even when she blocked his hits, they still ruined her balance and sent her careening backward. Every time she fell to the floor, Meredith kicked her the moment she got up.

Calling the fight one-sided would have been an understatement. This was little more than an act of assault.

I thought I could put up a fight…

Blood trickled down Sybilla's forehead. Her arms were swollen from internal hemorrhaging, and her left pinkie and ring finger were broken and twisted the wrong way.

I had no idea he was so much stronger!

She cursed her miscalculation, but Meredith didn't give her time to stew in her regret. Using his saber as a distraction, he gave her a swift punch, getting a clean hit in on her cheek and sending her hurtling away. One of her molars broke, and blood flooded her mouth.

She couldn't even flee. The other Vanajin members had circled around to cut off her escape route.

Miné had been watching from the side, and she laughed uproariously at Sybilla's predicament. She was already back on her feet. The antidote had worked like a charm. "Ah-ha-ha. C'mon, boss, can't we just shoot her already?"

"That won't be necessary," Meredith scolded her. "If one of the Crown's subjects somehow heard the shot, it would cause them undue fear."

So that was why he hadn't been using his gun. He didn't think he needed it.

"Squad F, go catch Flower Garden and Meadow. I'll capture this one and use her as a hostage."

On his order, nine of the agents dashed toward the building's entrance.

Sybilla rose to her feet and gave chase. "You ain't goin' nowhere!!" She took the knife she'd nearly dropped more times than she could count and clutched it tight.

Meredith stepped into her path to cut her off. "Not happening."

He thrust out his saber, and this time, she wasn't able to block.

The moment it touched her body, she felt her feet lift off the ground. She'd been sent off-balance like a wave of energy had just slammed her from the side.

Meredith's technique wasn't designed to slash or to stab. The tip of his saber shifted her charge's vector, and Sybilla rose into the air like she was doing a somersault before crashing spine-first into the ground. Another agonizing shock shot through her back. She rolled gracelessly to the side, then struggled back to her feet.

"Ah-ha-ha, I'd surrender now if I were you," Miné said with a round of applause and a mocking sneer. "We've already gotten your measure. Isn't it about time you wised up?" No matter how many times Sybilla had to listen to her, she never got less grating. "You're leagues weaker than 'Flash Fire' Monika. You're practically an amateur. In what world did you think you could ever match her?!"

"______"

Sybilla had tried to turn her eyes from the truth, but it was getting thrown right in her face.

There was a history to Monika and Sybilla's power dynamic.

Nobody ever said it out loud, but it was obvious to anyone with eyes that Sybilla simply wasn't as strong in a fight as Monika. The two of them fulfilled similar roles on the team—they were there for when things got violent. However, there was a gap between them that no amount of effort could fill.

That wasn't to say that Sybilla was a slouch. In a fair fight on level ground with weapons banned, she could probably take Monika in a fight. She had a deep well of stamina, and she always pulled her weight on the team.

However, *Monika's skills were downright unreal.*

There wasn't a person on Lamplight who denied that Monika's instincts were on a whole different level. Her marksmanship was unparalleled, and her ability to take advantage of light and ricochets allowed her to bamboozle her foes. Plus, she'd improved dramatically during their time in the Fend Commonwealth. She'd even driven off the mighty Klaus.

There was a time once when Klaus had taken Monika on a mission and left Sybilla behind. She was a member of the Unchosen Squad, and Klaus had made the right decision putting her there.

Sybilla was reminded of that painful truth all over again as she continued battling Meredith. She'd finished buying the time she needed, but she still couldn't afford to stop fighting back.

However, she couldn't see any path to victory.

Before she knew it, she'd redirected all her efforts from attacking to simply defending herself. If she wasn't retreating, she was taking a tumble, and whenever their blades crossed, she was always the one who came off the exchange with fresh wounds.

Sybilla couldn't beat Monika, and Monika had failed to beat Meredith. She could feel the relationship between those two inequalities bouncing around in her head.

"You think I don't know that shit?!"

If there was one thing Sybilla had over Monika, however, it was that she refused to accept when she was beat.

She grabbed onto Meredith's right arm, the one holding his saber. They'd exchanged enough blows by then that she was starting to get a read on his moves. She could pick up on the patterns of how he breathed before each attack.

Meredith tried to wrestle himself free, but Sybilla caught his left hook with her right arm.

"She blocked that?!" Miné gasped.

Meredith let out a sharp breath.

Sybilla held his arm and refused to let go, pinning him down with the three working fingers on her left hand. "Look, I get that Monika's hot shit an' all…"

She built up strength in her right hand, the one with the knife.

She was summoning every ounce of combat prowess she'd built up in her training with Klaus.

"…but I came here to turn those power rankings on their GOD-DAMN HEADS!"

"And what of it?"

There was a shift in Meredith's movements.

In a blink, he escaped Sybilla's grip and dipped backward. Where earlier he'd been tracing circular arcs in the air with his saber, now he shifted gears completely and came straight at her.

When he did, *the tip of his blade pierced Sybilla's right shoulder.*

"Wh———?"

Everything froze.

The knife tumbled from her hand and clattered to the floor with a dull *clang.*

"But I thought…you weren't about stabbing…?"

"Did you seriously believe that?"

Meredith gave her a pitying look and wrenched his saber free from her shoulder. Pain radiated from the wound.

She clutched her shoulder and screamed.

She'd never felt anything like this before in her life, and she writhed on the ground in agony. She bit down on her lip, but no matter how hard she tried to fight through it, she couldn't move her body. Instead, she just lay there enduring the pain as her head drooped on the ground in a pathetic semblance of a bow.

"We're done here." She could Meredith's icy voice come from above her. "Stop resisting, and I'll spare your life. I have questions for you."

"———"

It was almost funny how badly she'd been thrashed. That hadn't even been a proper fight. At no point had Meredith been taking her seriously. Not once had he used his gun, gone for her vitals with his saber, or called on his agents to back him up. Yet in spite of all that, she hadn't even lasted five minutes.

What the hell, man? And here I was, thinkin' I'd gotten stronger…

Her lips quivered in chagrin.

But I haven't gotten shit! I look like an absolute fuckin' chump!

Her body was riddled with wounds, and she could feel sweat and grit seeping into the broken skin. That pain made the facts crystal clear. Klaus could've won. Monika could've put up a better fight. But her? She'd gotten annihilated. She'd failed to put so much as a scratch on Meredith, she was hunched over like a caterpillar, and Meredith held her life in his hands. It was pathetic; there was no other word for it. Her teammates had overcome powerful foes, yet here she was, just as weak as ever.

"Hmph. The battlefield is no place for crying children." Meredith sighed and stowed his saber back in its scabbard. "Let me tell you why it is you'll never beat me."

"........."

"Your infantile feelings of rivalry toward Flash Fire dull your movements. You think you can do anything she can, and it makes you overplay your hand like a fool." When Meredith went on, he did so in a bellow loud enough it nearly shook the building. "Everything we do, we do for the Crown. If you thought that self-interested blade of yours could reach us, then think again!"

"..........................."

Sybilla had yet to lift her head from the ground, but when Meredith's angry roar washed over her, her eyes went wide.

◇◇◇

Now that he mentioned it, it should have been obvious that this was how things would play out.

The CIM had taken some embarrassing defeats courtesy of their Serpent mole, but their individual agents still boasted considerable potential. Even if Sybilla and Lily had been fighting together, there was no way they'd be able to match up to a CIM officer.

Sybilla's fighting skills had a whole other level to them. However, she herself was unaware of that, and it was a level she'd yet to attain. She wouldn't be able to until she properly confronted her past.

The CIM had Lamplight surrounded, and they weren't going to be able to break through.

As a result, they wouldn't be able to get to Klaus, and another tragedy was going to rear its ugly head.

There was just one person who could prevent that from happening. One person who could turn it all around...

"I just remembered somethin'," she murmured.

It wasn't the embarrassment of being scolded by her opponent in the middle of a fight that had led her to her revelation. And it wasn't the hints of sympathy that had crept into Meredith's voice as the seasoned spy had shouted at his novice counterpart, either. No, there was something that had stirred her heart more than her feelings of humiliation and powerlessness.

"There's another guy who told me the same things you just did."

Meredith regarded her with suspicion. "What are you talking about?"

His agents frowned as well. They could sense that there was something different about the way she was babbling.

Sybilla ignored them all. "He said it in the most annoying way, too. He was all like, 'Don't go obsessing over your academy grades. ♪'" She looked up and smiled. "But the funny thing is, he let himself get pinned down by those same narrow rankings he was talkin' about. There was this dude on his team he couldn't beat, and it drove him nuts. His teammate was a prodigy, and this guy just couldn't keep up."

She exhaled.

"He's the one who taught me that one of my key weapons was bein' able to coordinate with others."

How did it feel when he passed that wisdom onto her? she wondered.

The man had trained like his life depended on it. He'd honed his social skills, his combat skills, anything he could find to add to his arsenal. Yet even after all that, he still couldn't beat Avian's boss, Vindo.

Just as Sybilla was no match for Monika, *he* was no match for Vindo.

Oh, damn, Sybilla thought, *I never realized we had that in common.*

Meredith frowned at her, annoyed by the fact that he had no idea what she was referring to. "Who are you even talking about—"

"THE GUY YOU FUCKERS KILLED!!"

Meredith let out a growl, and all the agents in the room, Miné included, gasped.

Then there was a sound from overhead—from the second floor of the building they were in. It sounded like something was shaking.

"What was that?" someone cried, and Meredith looked up at the ceiling.

Sybilla smiled and thought about "Lander" Vics—Avian's combat specialist with a sharp tongue and bad habit of poking fun at people. Vics had once boasted the second-best marks out of the entire academy population. He was so handsome he could have passed as a movie star, and he thought little of most of the people around him.

He was also freakishly strong, a fact that Sybilla had learned when she battled him back in Longchon. He'd spent the entirety of their exchange period harassing Sybilla and dragging her to group dates, but he'd also taught her plenty about how to fight as a spy.

She thought back to the time she spent with him and spoke with conviction. "I'm no match for this guy. I need your help, Vics."

Her legs felt like they were about to give out under her, but she stood back up all the same.

"We're Lander and Pandemonium—and it's time to get smashing and clean 'em out."

Up on the second floor, a pair of spies smiled as they listened to the conversation taking place on the floor below.

"Look, Vics, she's cooounting on you," drawled "Feather" Pharma. She had long, wavy hair and a well-rounded figure. She looked like the very embodiment of sloth. She sat down on the window frame and gazed outside to savor the special night. "But who can blame her? They're not strong enough yet, not enough to overcome the CIM. I mean, they even needed my help seeing through Miiiné's lie."

"Lander" Vics gave her a shrug. "You're telling me. I swear, we can't leave them on their own for a second. ♪"

Vics walked across the floor, scanning it as though searching for something before finally coming to a stop when he found it.

He took out his concealed brass knuckles and held them up high.

* * *

"You and me, Sybilla—let's do this. Just this once, I'll lend you a hand. ♪"

Then, with strength unbefitting his gentle features, he began smashing his target to bits.

When Sybilla stood back up, Meredith glared at her, flabbergasted. "What the hell are you talking about, girl?"

It was hard to blame him for his confusion. Sybilla was in no state to fight anymore. Her dominant hand was too weak to even hold a knife, and if she didn't stanch her impaled shoulder soon, she was liable to bleed out.

The fight had long since been decided.

By all rights, what she should have been doing was throwing herself on the CIM's mercy and giving them every last bit of intel she had—either that or trying to kill herself to carry out her duty as a spy and protect her nation's secrets.

"You really thought that bluff would work? Everyone on Avian except Cloud Drift is supposed to be dead." He blinked in bewilderment. "Coordinating with others? Don't make me laugh. You don't have any allies left."

"Sure I do," Sybilla shot back. "Us and Avian, we're in this together."

She didn't move. She just stood tall with her feet planted on the ground and gave Meredith an intense stare.

Meredith let out an exasperated sigh. "I pity you. You're so far gone you can't even think straight." He unhurriedly drew his saber back out of its scabbard. Then he took aim at Sybilla's left shoulder and got ready to unleash another piercing thrust. "Finishing you will be a mercy. You and your ghosts *will* submit."

That was when *the ceiling broke.*

"——?!"

Meredith froze mid-windup.

The awful sound of rock cracking sounded out, and a moment later, the ceiling came thundering down on them. Plaster, concrete, and bundles of electrical wire descended from above.

Sybilla was already on the move. She dodged the rubble and charged across the room.

"B-but why?!"

Meredith acted fast, too. Rather than attacking, he devoted his full attention toward protecting his people. Some of his agents were slow to react, and he tackled them over toward the safety of the room's pillars.

When the ceiling finished collapsing, right when he tried to go check his remaining agents' safety, the onrushing figure seized her opportunity. Sybilla had circled into his blind spot during the disaster, and she threw an object at her distracted foe.

Acting fast, Meredith blocked it with a deft bit of swordsmanship.

The object turned out to be a perfume bottle. Meredith's saber smashed through the glass with ease.

The liquid inside splashed all over his face.

"Rgh, poison?!"

Right before Lily bailed, she'd slipped Sybilla a bottle.

Meredith fell back and wiped his face. A few drops had gotten in his mouth. He grimaced.

"You forget, I've the antidote right—"

By the time he'd opened his eyes, Sybilla was already bearing down on him. She was too close for him to use his saber. She stretched her mangled left hand toward him.

"All I gotta do is steal it—"

"NOT ON MY WATCH!"

Meredith launched a hook at her.

His fist slammed into her side. He'd put all his strength into it, and the blow was a heavy one. It lifted her off the ground, then sent her rolling across the floor like a ball before smashing into a nearby pillar.

"One last act of defiance, huh? Perhaps there's more to you than meets the eye." He let out an impressed sigh. "I don't know how you did it, but you brought down the ceiling somehow and used that opening to get poison into my system. I can see you planned to seal the deal by stealing my antidote...but that was where you failed."

The perfume bottle in Meredith's pocket was still safe and sound. He gulped down the tea inside it. It was the smart call, taking the antidote before the poison even had a chance to kick in.

After finishing off the bottle in a single swig, he gave his mouth a triumphant wipe with his hand. "Are we finally finished now? I really do need to get this interrogation started."

Sybilla didn't have the strength left to flee. She was sitting with her back to the pillar, her head slumped, and her legs outstretched.

"I really am good for nothin'."

Her voice had no life in it.

There was blood streaming down her right arm, and two of the fingers on her left hand were broken. Her shredded clothes did little to hide her battered skin.

"And I really am no match for Monika. Shit sucks, but there's no sense denyin' it."

She slowly raised her head.

Her face was sullied with blood and tears, but her smile was plain as day.

"I can't even fool someone without coordinatin' with my team to make it happen."

Meredith froze.

He immediately knew what had happened. His eyes went wide.

"———!!"

The thing was, that wasn't the antidote he just drank.

In the middle of their fight, *Sybilla had stolen his antidote and swapped it out for a bottle full of poison.*

Stealing things was what Pandemonium did best. Her new technique took her ability to divert her opponent's attention and steal their things and reversed it so she could plant things on their person as well.

However, it wasn't a move she could pull off solo. Sybilla didn't have the brains to deceive her foes. If Lily hadn't prepped the poison back there, Sybilla's plan would have been dead on arrival.

She borrowed, she lent, and she shared. Her liecraft was born from coordinating with her teammates.

Theft × Replacement = Two Truths and a Lie.

That was poison Meredith just drank, not antidote. And it wasn't the watered-down stuff Miné had gotten hit with. He might have gotten a few drops of antidote in his mouth earlier, but that was nothing compared to the amount of raw poison he'd just imbibed.

He doubled over.

"Don't tell me that this was your plan all along—"

"We're Flower Garden and Pandemonium—and it's time to bloom out of control and clean 'em out."

As Sybilla said the name of her absent teammate, she broke into a grin.

"I just swapped it."

With that, the mighty foe that had forced even Monika to retreat lay prone before her.

As soon as Meredith's large frame toppled over, the other Vanajin members came charging in. Sybilla's body was broken, and the other agents were intent on finishing her off.

Sure enough, victory was beyond her. Her defeat was written in stone.

Now, though, she could at least open a dialogue.

"No one move!" She held up her left hand. "One more step, and I smash the antidote."

In it, she was holding the vial with the antidote.

As far as threats went, that one held weight. The Vanajin agents froze. Even if they tried to shoot her, the impact from her dropping the vial would be enough to break it, too.

"I need you all to listen. There really is a mole in the CIM. We had nothin' to do with Tunekeeper's agent gettin' murdered!" she cried. "Who'd the report come from? Your team, or someone else?!"

She still didn't have any evidence she could show them to back her story up. However, the balance of power had shifted. Right now, she held their superior officer's life in her hands. Protecting confidential information was their job, sure, but there was no way they would just cut their boss loose at a moment's notice.

"ANSWER ME!" The blood loss was making her head go fuzzy, but she gritted her teeth and raised her voice. "What are you people plotting?!"

In the end, it was Meredith who spoke. "Weren't Lamplight the ones who tried to fool us first?" he grunted through the pain. "We have intel suggesting that Bonfire has ties to Serpent. I saw the evidence myself."

"...What?"

"That's why Miné was secretly getting ready to take you out."

Sybilla was struck speechless at how outrageous the accusation was. Was *that* what the CIM believed?

"There's no way. That doesn't even make sense..."

"Show me some proof that the claims are unfounded, then. You could just be lying to save your own skin—"

"If I cared about savin' my skin, I wouldn't have fought you and gotten stabbed through the fuckin' arm!"

When Sybilla shouted, Meredith nodded like it had all just clicked into place for him. "Right." He bit down on his lip in frustration. "It would seem we've all been played for fools. That's odd. Mr. Nathan should have been able to spot the lie..."

He still had reservations, but it would appear that he'd figured out who the traitor was.

"Who was it? Who's the one spreadin' that bullshit?"

As soon as Meredith told her the name, a mechanical sound buzzed from his pocket. He was getting a message on his radio. The buzzing was soon followed by someone's voice.

Once it was over, Meredith gave Sybilla a grave look.

"One of my agents just reported in. Bonfire disappeared from his holding cell."

"——?!"

Gathering the last of her strength in her legs, Sybilla leaped at him.

"What you do you think you're doing?" the Vanajin agents cried. They rushed in to try to capture her, but she tossed them the antidote and ripped the radio out of Meredith's pocket. "I gave Miné's radio to Lily and Sara! How do I contact 'em?"

Meredith immediately picked up on what she was getting at. "Show her," he ordered the others.

As soon as Miné showed Sybilla how to operate the special CIM radio, she immediately shouted into it. "Lily, Sara!! Do you read me?!"

Lily's voice promptly crackled back. *"Sybilla?! Are you okay?!"*

"I'm fine, but that's not important," she replied. "What's the situation on your end?"

"Right, yeah, it's bad! Teach isn't here in the building anymore! The Belias agents who were guarding him have no idea what's going on!"

The good news was, the others had successfully reached their destination. Right before they went in to save Klaus, though, they'd noticed that something was off about his guards.

"W-we just spotted a shady-looking car drive off, so we're circling back to your position. It's so dark and foggy that—"

"Follow that car!!" Sybilla bellowed at the top of her lungs.

The way things stood, there was a very real chance that the two of them might be the only ones capable of catching up to Klaus. If nothing else, Sybilla wasn't going to be able to help in the mission anymore.

"Huh?"

"The bad guys beat us to the punch! Whatever you do, don't lose that car!! White Spider's mole is—"

She told them the name, but that was her breaking point. It had been a long time coming, but her consciousness finally slipped away. Mortified and frustrated, she left the rest in her teammates' hands.

An automobile raced through the foggy night.

Its engine was so quiet, it was nearly silent. That was due to special tech, no doubt of the CIM's design.

Klaus turned to the woman sitting beside him in the back seat. "So what's the big deal? Why am I getting transferred?"

He'd been ordered out of his holding cell just ten minutes prior. After being told to put his arms behind his back so they could handcuff him with a full five new sets of shackles, they'd ushered him into a car.

No one had told Klaus anything about the transfer ahead of time. He was the bait designed to lure out White Spider, so it made little sense to move him.

He shot a glare at the woman who'd dragged him there. "And with only a pair of guards on my detail, no less. You're really keeping a tight lid on this operation."

"There's been an emergency," Amelie replied bluntly. "I'll fill you in on the details later."

She said little, and she was holding her gun at the ready. If Klaus tried to resist, she would shoot him on the spot.

At the moment, he had little choice but to go along with her orders.

For the last several days, Klaus hadn't received a single bit of information from the outside world. The CIM hadn't left so much as a newspaper in his holding cell. He had no grasp of what the situation at large looked like, and he had no basis with which to argue against her orders.

It was nearly ten at night, and the city of Hurough was shrouded in fog. Eventually, the car turned onto a factory lot. There were train tracks leading out from the building. It was a garage where they repaired locomotives.

The car pulled up alongside a steam locomotive.

The locomotive was massive. It looked like a huge black pillar that had been knocked onto its side. That was how they made them in the Fend Commonwealth.

"The steam locomotive was born right here in this nation, you know," Amelie said, suddenly feeling talkative. "Some forty years ago, we exported them to your very own Din Republic. What do you think? This one boasts the traditional elegance of my nation's 4-6-0 wheel arrangement, and its boiler can reach over seventeen kilos of pressure. I don't imagine the Republic has anything that compares."

"You sound oddly proud about that. I never took you for such a rail buff."

"I'm allowed to have a hobby or two," she replied, sounding a little embarrassed. She nodded toward the train. "We're getting on."

Doing so would allow them to transport him in utmost secrecy.

Behind the train itself, there were a pair of passenger cars hooked to its back. Bright lights were visible through the cracks in their windows.

There was no platform, so they had to use a ladder to board the train. That said, climbing a ladder without being able to use his hands proved rather challenging. "Please, I'm sure this is nothing to you," Amelie prodded him, and he eventually managed to keep his balance long enough to get on board.

The driver who brought them there didn't join them, and once Klaus and Amelie got in the passenger car, the locomotive began moving. Klaus couldn't see them, but he assumed the train was operating on a skeleton crew. As he understood it, a train needed a minimum of two people in order to run—an engineer to drive, and a stoker to manage its power. They must have been up in the engine room.

After the train got moving, it quickly picked up speed. In what seemed like no time at all, it cleared the factory and linked up with the standard rail network.

At this speed, jumping off won't be an option.

Once the train hit sixty miles an hour, jumping off with his arms bound would be suicide, even for him.

Klaus looked at the scenery outside the window and got to work analyzing the situation. Escaping the train wouldn't be possible, not unless it stopped. And he couldn't expect any help from the outside, either.

He sat down in one of the passenger seats and let out a sigh. "You really wanted some alone time with me, didn't you?"

"That's right. I did." Amelie didn't deny it. She sat down in a separate row from Klaus and looked straight ahead. "I wanted to share my answer with you." Her lips parted. "As I recall, you were the one who advised me to question everything I knew."

That does sound familiar, Klaus mused. It was back when the two of them were searching for Monika. The double whammy of losing Belias to Lamplight and discovering that there was a traitor in the CIM had left her reeling, and Klaus had told her that as an inconsequential piece of advice to a colleague.

"I've been thinking about that a lot these past few days. And I've been watching the way you all fight." She continued staring straight ahead. “The only desire I ever had was to protect this beautiful country that Her Majesty the Queen rules over and where family and loved ones live in peace. I asked myself, what was the best way to achieve that? Should I really just keep my head down and follow my orders? Is that the right thing to do? The thought was never far from my mind.”

“Did you find an answer?”

“I did.” Amelie’s expression softened. “And I made the same decision as your mentor.”

Before Klaus had a chance to ask her what she meant by that, the passenger car’s door slid open, and a man came in from the engine room. He was holding a gun in his hand and walking with a spring in his step.

“Been a while since I saw you in the flesh, ya monster.”

His was a face Klaus would never forget. That was the Serpent member who made a traitor of his mentor, who wrecked Inferno, and who eventually shot Klaus’s mentor dead. And to top it all off, he’d led Klaus’s pupil Monika to ruin.

Klaus gave the man a murderous look. “White Spider.”

“This’ll be one for the history books.” White Spider stuck out his tongue. “It’s the day that Inferno finally dies.”

Chapter 4
The Status Quo

"Puppeteer" Amelie had devoted herself to her nation.

She was recruited as a student for her outstanding talent and became a counterintelligence agent for the CIM. Belias, the team she would one day run, was a special unit that answered directly to the agency's senior leadership. Many of her missions were extremely confidential. She investigated major politicians suspected of treason, detained journalists who had dirt on the royal family, and carried out countless other operations as well. Not once did she ever question her orders. She was a loyal foot soldier, and she did whatever she was told. After all, she herself was nothing more than another puppet.

Everything she did, she did for her beloved homeland. For the Crown. For the sake of the peace her old family and lover were able to enjoy.

One day, though, that loyalty was used against her, and she was forced to reevaluate her entire life. Her superior Green Butterfly ordered her to attack Avian, so attack them she did. Foreign spies or not, the raid was entirely unjustified. Amelie kept on following the bad intel, and it ultimately resulted in her failing to protect Prince Darryn, suffering a humiliating defeat at Lamplight's hands, and getting detained alongside her entire team.

Through their actions, Klaus, Sybilla, Erna, and Monika had all opened her eyes. A mere foot soldier had no power to protect their nation. She was no slave. She was a spy, and she needed to figure out what it was her nation needed from her.

Ironically, the person who pointed her in the right direction was Green Butterfly, the very person who'd tricked her in the first place.

"There's a man you could meet who'd give you aaaaall the answers you're looking for," Green Butterfly told her. It was like she'd seen right through Amelie's uncertainty. "He's a coward, though, so he might not show up if you don't go alone."

Fortunately, there was nobody there to hear Green Butterfly but her.

Amelie didn't hesitate. She knew that this was part of Green Butterfly's scheme, but she needed to take her destiny in her own hands.

As she waited at the designated pier in the dead of night, she sensed someone nearby. Just as Green Butterfly had warned her, the man was cautious. He took nearly half an hour carefully sounding out the area to make sure that it wasn't a trap and that Amelie didn't have people lying in wait.

Eventually, a man with terrible posture showed himself. "Damn, Green Butterfly's really pulling her weight. CIM senior leadership knows how to pick 'em," he said. "Tell me, my fair lady, what is your heart's desire?"

"I want to know everything." Amelie stood up straight. "I want to know what Serpent and Inferno were fighting for, and I want to know what sin Prince Darryn was sullying his hands with. I want to have all the facts when I make my decision."

The man gave her a vaguely disquieting smile. "Don't you worry," he said, his voice familiar and barely louder than a whisper. "I always side with the underdog."

The train didn't slow down as it made its way out of Hurough proper. Its wheels screeched every so often, causing the whole carriage to shake.

Klaus slowly rose to his feet so he could step into the aisle and face White Spider.

"Someone like you could never understand how she feels." White

Spider shot a quiet look over at Amelie. "But me, I respect her. She learned what it meant to lose, she started doubting the things everyone around her took for granted, and she drew her own conclusions. The way I see it, people who use their failures as opportunities to grow are the biggest badasses there are."

Amelie stood up as well and took a spot beside White Spider. Standing by his side as though to demonstrate her new allegiance, she held her gun at the ready and glared at Klaus. She'd been masking her hostility on the ride over, but now her intent was crystal clear.

White Spider shrugged. "And just for the record, I don't know how to brainwash people or anything."

"It's true. I joined Serpent of my own volition." There was no hesitation in Amelie's eyes. "This is me carrying out my duty. I can say that with my head held high."

This was the most confident Klaus had ever seen her. She was no longer the woman blindly following Hide's orders or panicking when her team was taken hostage. Everything about her practically radiated conviction.

White Spider and Amelie had teamed up to kill him.

Seeing that laid out for him in black and white caused a lump to form in Klaus's throat. Although he didn't hold any particular affection for Amelie, the two of them had still spent no small number of hours working together. Betrayal might have been a fact of life for spies, but that never made it sting any less.

The train car had been sequestered from the rest of the world, and that was where they were going to gun him down.

"Why?" he asked. "What was it that changed you? When you shed those tears for Prince Darryn's death in public, was that all a lie? The man you're standing beside is the one who killed him, you know."

Amelie's expression didn't waver. She'd long since made up her mind.

However, Klaus still needed to say it.

"It's not too late to—"

"Of course it's too late."

It was White Spider who gave the response. He flicked his gun and pulled the trigger without a moment's hesitation. At no point had Klaus seen him draw a bead, yet his bullet flew with unerring accuracy all the same—*and blasted through Amelie's head.*

It wasn't Klaus he'd shot, but his own ally standing beside him.

Amelie's body went flying.

The bullet had gone straight through her skull, and blood came exploding out of her head. As her body crumpled to the floor, the frills of her dress were slowly stained red.

"Amelie...," Klaus gasped.

"Don't you dare judge me for that. She knew the stakes." White Spider shook his head in disappointment. Amelie's body didn't move. Anyone could have seen that she died on the spot. "If you pulled off some miracle and changed her mind, that would've been game over. Gotta cover all my bases, y'know?"

"———"

Those were the kinds of cold, hard decisions that spies had to make. There was a chance that Amelie might double-cross him and go side with Klaus, and White Spider had killed her for no reason other than to eliminate that possibility.

Amelie knew what she was getting herself into. She knew that spies who turned traitor didn't generally get to live happily ever after. But still, what kind of person would...

No. Klaus shook his head. He couldn't afford to let his emotions cloud his judgment.

Some blood had splattered on White Spider's face, and he wiped it away with his hand. "Now I've got you alone, you freak."

"Indeed you do."

In a sense, Klaus had been hoping for this. Standing before him was the man he wanted to kill more than anyone else. He hated to admit it, but White Spider was essentially his nemesis. For half a year now, Klaus had thought about little other than capturing him, interrogating him, and squeezing the life from his body. That was the man who'd stolen Klaus's family, Inferno, from him. That was the man who'd destroyed Avian and Monika.

"I gotta say, it took a whole lotta work getting here." White Spider had been waiting for this moment, too. He gave a pleased shrug. "Now I can finally avenge Silver Cicada. I'll make sure to plant your head on her grave."

"...What?"

That was a name he hadn't heard before.

White Spider arched an eyebrow. "Whaddya mean, what?"

"Who's Silver Cicada?"

"...Okay, really? You could've figured that out. Remember how we sent Purple Ant after your boss and stuff? Well, we sent someone to kill you, too. A chick named Silver Cicada."

"Ah, I see."

"Shouldn't it have been obvious? Like, from context?"

"I'm pretty sure you're just bad at explaining things."

Klaus was caught by surprise; he hadn't even been aware there was a grudge involved.

That said, he did have some idea of who White Spider was talking about. Around the time he now believed Inferno was getting taken out, Klaus had been through a brutal ordeal of his own. Not only had his body broken down for reasons unknown, but he'd been attacked by a series of assassins. Klaus had turned the tables on each and every one of them, but he'd done so by narrow enough margins that he hadn't been able to interrogate them and learn their names. Apparently, one of them had been a member of Serpent.

Returning to the topic at hand, he gave White Spider another head-on stare. "I have the same question I asked you before."

"What's that?"

"Why did my mentor betray Inferno?" It was the question he'd posed to White Spider back in the Din Republic entertainment district. "I know you people aren't just acting at random. You have something you believe in. And it's something so important it was enough to win my mentor and Amelie over."

"I'll give you the same answer I did back then." The smile faded from White Spider's lips. "If I told you the whole truth, would you join Serpent?"

"....................."

There was a sincerity in his voice that made Klaus realize he was asking the question in earnest. If Klaus said yes, White Spider might very well tell him everything. As a spy, the right thing for Klaus to do here would be to offer him an empty promise in order to drag information out of him.

However, that was the one thing Klaus refused to do. Not because it was the incorrect move, but because every instinct he had was rejecting the notion flat-out. Perhaps it was immature of him, and perhaps he deserved to be mocked for his decision, but he knew that to ignore that impulse would go against everything he was as a person.

"It doesn't make sense. Why do you hate Serpent so much?" White Spider frowned in exasperation. "Your own mentor, Guido, joined us. Why can't you believe in him? It's not like I threatened him or anything. You really think I could've forced that murder machine to do anything he didn't want to?" The reverence in his voice was impossible to miss. "Up to the bitter end, Guido was never ashamed of the choices he'd made."

"You don't get to talk about my mentor."

When at last Klaus finally showed some emotion, that emotion was fury.

He refused to accept it. There was no way that Guido—his mentor, the man he thought of as a father—had chosen to walk the same path as White Spider.

There was no room for compromise here. Klaus was simply going to beat the information he needed out of White Spider.

"Nothing you say or do could ever make me join Serpent."

"All right. Them's the breaks, I guess." White Spider shook his head like he'd seen this coming all along. He raised his gun, squared his shoulders, and took aim with both hands.

This was a man who'd achieved pinpoint accuracy while firing one-handed. This was not a shot he was going to miss.

"You need to die." His voice was almost pleading. "If I don't kill you now, you're going to become a menace to the entire world. A sinner with the blood of millions on your hands."

Klaus had no idea what he was talking about, and he doubted his foe intended to elaborate.

White Spider placed his finger on the trigger.

"The sentence for that is death."

Klaus tensed his arms behind his back.

Unfortunately, his bindings held strong. The five sets of manacles had been fixed firmly in place. Not even dislocating his joints would be enough to slip free. Amelie would never have used restraints that could be undone so easily.

It went without saying that without his arms, he had no meaningful ability to use weapons. All he could do was move his legs, one of which was injured. However, fleeing wasn't an option. The train was moving too fast for him to safely leap off.

As he finished reviewing the situation, something welled up inside him.

That something was laughter.

"Heh."

"Huh?"

A single laugh escaped Klaus's mouth. Once the dam broke, though, there was no going back. He shook with mirth as he let out uninhibited peals of laughter.

"Haaaaaa-ha-ha-ha-ha-ha-ha! Heh, heh, ha-ha-ha! Bwa-ha-ha-ha! Ah-ha-ha-ha-ha! Ha-ha! Ha-ha! Heh-heh-heh! Ah-ha-ha-ha! Ha-ha-ha-haaaaa!"

The sound of his voice filled the entire carriage.

His stomach hurt from how hard he was laughing. It had been years since the last time that happened.

"What's so funny?" White Spider spluttered. "I never took you for someone who would laugh so hard…"

It was true. Under normal circumstances, the idea of Klaus laughing like that would be unthinkable. However, the situation was simply too hilarious for him not to.

"So this was your plan, White Spider? This was you bringing your full might to bear?"

"What…?"

"When I think about how much of your life you spent, how much effort you poured into this, I just…I can't help but laugh."

Along with the laughter, Klaus felt a profound sense of emptiness. How many people had devoted themselves to bringing this moment about? Scores of people like Avian and Amelie had lost their lives for this. Countless elite spies had scurried across the globe burning through untold sums of money. And at the end of it all, *this* was what White Spider had to show for it? This paltry excuse for a trap?

"By the way, I have to ask—"

Klaus spoke the words like he was letting out a sigh.

"—how much longer should I keep playing along with this game?"

White Spider's eyes went wide. His expression was one of complete and utter confusion.

White Spider stood motionless, his gun still at the ready. Klaus was supremely confident, and it didn't look like he was bluffing.

What's going on? He can't use his arms, and he can barely move his left leg.

White Spider had ordered Amelie to completely lock down Klaus's arms, and she'd given him an up-to-date report on Klaus's injury. White Spider doubted she'd made any oversights.

No, but like, seriously, he's gonna die, right?

He pulled the trigger, as much to blow his own doubts away as anything.

His shot flew at Klaus, not erring in its course.

White Spider doubted that the first shot would be enough to finish him off. However, Klaus couldn't flee or fight back, so as long as White Spider pumped enough lead into him, he should—*should*—eventually die.

The bullet soared straight past Klaus.

After dodging it with the smallest of motions and allowing it to merely graze his temple, Klaus closed in on White Spider. White Spider fired a second shot, but Klaus twisted his body to avoid that one, too. His body rose into the air, and he fired off a dropkick so graceful you never would have known he had his arms bound behind his back.

"Wha—?"

White Spider brought up his arms to block the hit, but the impact was still staggering. His posture crumpled. He quickly rose back to his feet by rolling backward first, then readied his pistol again.

With just a single kick, Klaus had forced him all the way to the far end of the train car. The door leading to the engine room was locked from the inside. He had nowhere to run.

"I'm disappointed." Klaus stood there, resting his weight on his right leg so as not to overburden his left. "You turned my ally against me to wound my leg. You bound my arms. You took all my weapons. And you locked me in this closed space so I couldn't escape. You know, that all makes sense."

When he went on, every hair on White Spider's body stood on edge.

"But so what? You really thought that would be enough to beat me?"

Purely on impulse, White Spider fired another shot.

This isn't possible. What the hell is he even talking about?!

Klaus sprang up with his right leg alone and dodged the bullet.

That gave White Spider an opening to dash past him and put some more distance between them. He dashed all the way across the carriage, firing a shot aimed squarely at Klaus as he went.

However, it failed to find its mark.

Using his right leg as a fulcrum, Klaus spun his body and dodged the bullet by a hair's breadth.

You've gotta be fucking kidding me! How can he move like that with only one leg?!

Klaus was using the space they were in to its fullest potential. Using only his right leg, he kicked off the seats and walls with tight, precise steps as though to show how confident he was that he could dodge anything White Spider threw at him.

White Spider was certain of it now—Amelie hadn't screwed up at all. The man could barely use his arms or left leg. Bonfire was just enough of a monster that *one leg was all he needed.*

White Spider barreled from one end of the train car to the other, and Klaus ran with him on that one leg of his.

"Fuckin' shit!!" White Spider roared.

He was no novice when it came to fighting spies who knew how to dodge bullets. If they did, he simply updated his mental dossier on them, predicted their movements, and aimed his bullets at where they were about to be rather than where they were. The problem was, Klaus was on a whole different level. White Spider would be certain his shot had landed true, but right as his heart swelled with delight, Klaus would vanish. The way he was moving made it look like he was teleporting, like his entire body was shifting to the right.

Guido had warned White Spider about that technique. That was "Firewalker" Gerde's footwork—the moves that had once carried a sniper hailed as immortal across dozens of battlefields.

He can still use it, even on just one foot?!

White Spider hadn't factored any of that into his calculations, and every move he made was one step behind.

Klaus closed in on White Spider and feinted with a kick to obscure White Spider's vision. After crouching down low, he next went for a headbutt.

"........"

When Klaus's hard forehead smashed into White Spider's nose, it sent White Spider reeling off-balance.

"The girls set traps like this for me constantly," Klaus said coolly, "and every time, I turn the tables on them."

"——!"

There was a bitter truth that White Spider had no choice but to accept—that Klaus had grown stronger still. White Spider had begrudgingly admitted that Klaus was the Greatest Spy in the World on that day he defeated Purple Ant in Mitario, and his skills had clearly advanced since then.

White Spider was by no means a pushover when it came to fighting. He'd been trained by both Indigo Grasshopper and Guido, and he was confident that he could overpower your average spy with ease. Yet here he was, completely and utterly outmatched by a one-legged Klaus.

Was this guy he was fighting even really human?!

As White Spider fought to regain his balance, he threw out a desperate punch. However, Klaus blocked the hit with his shoulder, planted his right leg firmly on the ground, and used the energy from White Spider's attack to swivel around it before performing a one-legged leap into the air.

Klaus somersaulted through the air, and his acrobatic spin kick pulverized White Spider's jaw.

"RRRGH!"

A handful of White Spider's teeth clattered to the floor.

The sensation of his brain wobbling sent him down alongside them, forcing him to scuttle away from Klaus on all fours.

"You made one big oversight." Klaus just stood there, self-possessed and unhurried. "There was one situation I absolutely needed to avoid—the one where you failed to come after me."

"………"

It wasn't like the notion hadn't crossed White Spider's mind. As a matter of fact, that was exactly what Black Mantis had suggested he do. There was a reason why fleeing hadn't been an option for White Spider, but Klaus had no way of knowing that.

What exactly had Klaus been plotting?

"The CIM didn't want that, either. That's why Cursemaster and I teamed up. We wanted to give you the peace of mind you needed to make an attempt on my life," Klaus said, "so we agreed to take *no steps whatsoever* that might get in the way of your plan."

Now it all made sense. White Spider had wondered why everything had gone so smoothly. Apparently, it was because that was exactly how "Cursemaster" Nathan, one of the members of the CIM's senior leadership, had wanted it.

Klaus gave him a taunting tilt of the head. "What, did you seriously think you'd captured me on your own merits?"

"——!!"

White Spider bit down hard on his lip. He had no counterargument to make, and the grim situation he was now in was a testament to that.

"Of the two plans I prepared, I never imagined that the first one—the excellent plan that was easy to pull off and required next to no effort—would get the job done all on its own."

Klaus sprang back into motion. Unafraid of White Spider's gun, he charged in and closed the gap. White Spider's bullets curved around his body like they'd been preordained to do so.

Now White Spider understood. Now he knew what had made Klaus laugh.

When you got right down to it, Klaus hadn't taken any countermeasures whatsoever. Knowing that an assassin was gunning for him, he'd watched Lamplight and the CIM scurry around, and he'd done nothing. He simply sat there and relaxed.

And *that had been enough.*

White Spider had poured his heart and soul into making sure his assassination plan had all the angles covered, and that was all it had taken to ruin it.

It was no wonder Klaus hadn't been able to hold back his laughter.

"Hurry up and yield. I have no interest in entertaining this desperate show of resistance," Klaus spat. He kicked White Spider in the stomach. **"You disgust me!!"**

Each and every one of his blows was bringing him closer to death.

How is he doing this? This is goddamn unfair!

Was it rage that drove him? White Spider had killed Inferno, killed Avian, and hurt many of the Lamplight girls. Klaus may have only been on one leg, but his attacks were fiercer than any bullet, and the fury behind them was a sight to behold. If White Spider let his guard slip, he might get knocked clean out.

Fuck you. Do you have any idea how long I've waited for this? How much I'm carrying?!

The two of them were at point-blank range, but White Spider fired anyway. As he blocked the kick with his left arm, he squeezed the trigger with his right hand. All he needed to do was land a single shot. He fired again and again, growing more desperate each time.

Silver Cicada... Blue Fly... Purple Ant... It's on me to avenge them...

Klaus used one of the seats' backrests as a foothold, kicking off it to dodge the bullets.

White Spider went to shoot him out of the air, but when he did, he realized his blunder. His automatic held ten shots, and he'd burned through all of them. He needed to reload, and Klaus was never going to give him the time to do that.

"Shiiiiit!"

He tossed his gun aside to free up his right hand. He needed to focus on protecting himself. With his new battle plan set, he moved to intercept.

Klaus fired off a flying knee strike.

White Spider poured everything he had into blocking it, and as he did, he pulled something out of his pocket and hurled it. That something was a small metal tube about the size of his thumb—a miniature bomb.

Less than a second later, it went off. The explosion tore through White Spider and Klaus alike.

Klaus backed off, forced away by the impact from the blast. After tumbling across the ground, he rolled back onto his feet. "A suicide bombing?!"

"If bullets and fists won't get the job done, then what the hell choice do I have?"

For the first time, there was pain in Klaus's expression. He was bleeding from the chest where the shrapnel had hit him.

"Still, that smarts like a motherfucker."

White Spider was lying on his ass. The shrapnel had gotten him in both of his arms.

That bomb had been his last resort. He knew he couldn't use anything too powerful; anything stronger would have run the risk of damaging Klaus's restraints. Still, he'd successfully landed an attack. Klaus could probably have dodged it if White Spider had thrown it from a distance, but at close range, even though it meant getting himself caught in the blast, he'd finally wounded his foe. White Spider had even managed to guard his vitals with his arms, an option that Klaus didn't have.

He raised his voice, hoping to crush Klaus's spirit. "One of us is eating shit first, and it's not gonna be me."

After clashing with the man head-on like that, White Spider could feel it.

There was no doubt in White Spider's mind that if that man walked out of there alive, the Nostalgia Project would come to fruition. Millions of people would die, and only the strong would be able to survive in the world that ensued.

The question was, who could possibly stop the last survivor of Inferno? Serpent's boss didn't stand a chance, nor did Indigo Grasshopper. There wasn't a spy alive who did. No matter how much of White Spider's life he had to burn to put that monster down, it was a price he was happy to pay.

Over in the edge of his vision, he saw Klaus's eyes go wide and his body quiver. "The way you moved just now..."

"Seriously, that's what's got your nuts all twisted?" Apparently it was that, rather than the surprise bomb, that had shocked Klaus. When White Spider had switched over to close-quarters combat, he'd used the techniques he'd inherited. "In the end, Guido chose Serpent. Don't you forget that."

Guido fought like a tornado, a fact that White Spider had experienced firsthand. That man had put in so much work helping White Spider achieve his dream, and White Spider had nothing but reverence for him.

"The final pupil that Guido taught his techniques to was me. *Not you.*"

"........."

Klaus's eyes went wide, and his shoulders stiffened. He stared at White Spider with a pitch-black darkness in his eyes. White Spider had successfully dragged even more rage out of him. "You really," Klaus growled, "know how to get under my skin!!"

"You honor me, O senior pupil."

Klaus wasn't the only one who was livid. The way that Klaus kept professing his love for Guido yet rejecting everything he stood for and slaughtering Guido's fellow Serpent members pissed White Spider off. Why was he so against walking the same path as his mentor?

"Now, come at me. I'll kill your ass, I'll tear down the world's rules..."

White Spider raised his voice to encourage himself, and for the first time in their whole fight, he took a step forward.

"...AND I'LL INHERIT GUIDO'S WILL!!"

"You don't get to say his name."

White Spider readied his next bomb, prepared to put his life on the line to best his foe.

Meanwhile, Klaus leaped forward to face him and got in position to unleash a kick. His plan was to end White Spider's life once and for all with his next attack.

One way or another, this was going to be their final clash.

White Spider had used every plan he could think of to strip all freedom from his opponent, and Bonfire had intentionally gone in without a plan and had overcome his imprisonment through raw physical might.

In the end, what drew closed the curtain on the battle between those two titans of espionage…

"———————!!"
"———————?!"

…was neither Klaus nor White Spider, but a third party altogether.

It took both of them a good long while to comprehend what had happened. Klaus assumed White Spider had put some scheme into effect, and White Spider was afraid it was Klaus who'd pulled some trick out of his sleeve. Mighty as they were, neither of them had foreseen this turn of events.

The moment before the two of them clashed, a bullet tore through Klaus's right leg.

It had come from a completely unexpected direction. Klaus crumpled to his knee from the blow, and White Spider backed off to ensure his own safety.

As the sound of the shot echoed through the carriage, the two combatants turned in unison to look at where the surprise attack had come from.

"Amelie…?"

The name spilled from Klaus's mouth at the shocking sight.

Down in the pool of blood where she lay, Amelie was clutching a gun. Her body wasn't moving. However, the barrel of her gun was aimed squarely at Klaus.

Amelie had long since lost any ability to see or hear. All she could sense in that silent darkness were the faint vibrations traveling across the floor. The people who'd just been dashing throughout the carriage were still now.

I do have my pride, you know.

She could feel the life draining from her, but she smiled triumphantly all the same. Or rather, she would have, if the muscles in her face still worked.

She'd fired her shot at the person moving on one leg—Klaus.

He wasn't moving now. Her shot must have found its mark.

Amelie didn't regret the decisions she'd made. At no point did she ever have proof that White Spider would treat her with compassion after she turned traitor. She'd had an inkling he might end up shooting her dead. Yet through to the bitter end, she remained true to her desire—to protect her beautiful homeland. She was willing to do anything to achieve that end, even work with Serpent.

Dying here is my penance. Retribution from all those I've killed myself.

She knew that the one life she had would never be enough to balance those scales. The only person she was satisfying was herself. But she didn't care. As far as final moments went, landing a blow on the Greatest Spy in the World had to be up there.

I wonder, Bonfire, did that change your evaluation of me?

She didn't care about that either, of course. The opinions of others were none of her concern.

As she went to her death, she did so of her own volition, not as anyone else's puppet.

Klaus was unable to rise to his feet.

The bullet had passed straight through his calf and damaged the tendons he needed to move his leg. He couldn't even muster any strength in it.

Stuck kneeling on the ground, he stared at Amelie in shock.

She was still able to move...?

The attack had caught him completely unaware.

Did she really play dead so well that neither me nor White Spider were able to notice?

Klaus immediately dismissed the possibility. She had definitely been dead. Nobody could survive having their brains blown out from point-blank like that.

But then, *she came back.*

Even in the absence of mental activity, people's hearts continued beating for a short while, and given the right electrical stimuli, their muscles could move, too. The shock from getting shot could stop their brain activity, but random happenstance could start it back up and momentarily bring a corpse back to life.

It sounded like something out of a ghost story, but that was what had happened to Amelie. Her pride as a spy had brought about a miracle. She was well and truly dead now, but her final action had dramatically shifted the course of the fight.

"Ah-ha-ha-ha-ha-hahaha-haaaah-ha-ha-ha-ha!" White Spider cackled. "Holy *shit*, Amelie! You are one *hell* of a spy! Nothing but respect for you!"

Klaus wanted to be mad, but he had to admit it. He and White Spider had both completely underestimated her. "Puppeteer" Amelie was a uniquely talented counterintelligence agent who'd led spies from across the world to their doom in order to protect the Fend Commonwealth, and that final attack of hers was a heavier blow than Klaus could afford to take.

"Damn, man. I really do have the devil's own luck. It's the one thing I've got going for me." White Spider drummed his fingers on his face in delight. Beneath them, the look in his eyes was crazed. "There's no way you're still able to fight, not in that state."

"........."

Klaus wished more than anything that he could simply bluff and tell White Spider he was wrong. His right leg was unusable, so if he wanted to flee, he would have to do it with his yet-unhealed left leg. However, it was taking everything he had just to stay upright. If he jumped even a single time, he had zero confidence he would so much as land on his feet.

Death was upon him.

White Spider scooped up his gun, savoring his victory, and loaded in his spare magazine. Based on his gun's model, Klaus knew it held ten shots. There was no way he would be able to dodge all of them.

"Here's a one-gun salute for ya..."

White Spider fired at the ceiling like he wanted to make sure his bullets were really there.

"...to celebrate the moment where I break the status quo."

It was classic loser behavior, getting carried away the moment he realized the situation had turned in his favor. However, the fact was that that man had brought Klaus, the self-proclaimed World's Strongest, to his knees. His bizarrely intense obsession had carried him through.

Then a sound reached them from behind the train car. Something had just come down from above. White Spider didn't notice it. His own gunshot had been too loud for him to hear anything.

"It's not going to break," Klaus said from down on his knees. "Master didn't teach you anything, did he? You can't break the status quo."

White Spider's grin faded. "What're you on about? Got some final words for me?"

"There's only one kind of person who shapes the rules like that. The strong. Nobody's going to lend an ear to the ramblings of a weakling."

"I'm telling you, that's exactly what I'm here to change—"

"You can't. You lack the conviction."

White Spider bit down ever-so-slightly on his lip.

That was the reaction of a man who'd been told the same thing before, and Klaus had a pretty good idea of who that might be.

"Ah. Master told you the same thing, didn't he?"

"——"

Upon seeing the scowl cross White Spider's face, Klaus could tell that his deduction had been true.

A feeling of warmth rose up in his chest. Guido may have been a traitor, but he'd still been Guido.

"You've got it all wrong," Klaus said, his heart tranquil. "Master wasn't saying that you needed to make mistakes, embrace your weakness, and sacrifice everything in pursuit of your goal. Conviction like that is cheap."

A masochistic smile crossed his face.

"Do you really think I've never lost or made mistakes?"

He may have called himself the World's Strongest, but he'd been doing so for less than a year. He hadn't always been that way, not from the start. He'd never won a fair fight against Guido, the boss scolded him constantly, and he'd whined and complained the whole way through Gerde's training. Every member on Inferno had strengths that Klaus couldn't hope to compete with.

"I've lost more in my life than I've gained. But even so, I keep putting one foot in front of the other. Even when I'm beaten, even when I fail, I never stop believing in my own potential."

His voice rang true.

"The only people who have the right to change the world…are those with the conviction to see themselves as strong."

Beside him, the carriage's rear door swung open.

Klaus didn't even have to look. He knew she'd made it.

This was his second plan—the terrible one that was next to impossible to pull off and carried nothing but risks and costs. Klaus and Cursemaster had taken zero measures to stop White Spider. It was clear that White Spider had carried out his plan and that his traitor had thrown the CIM into turmoil. Yet even so, even in spite of that, Klaus still believed that the girls would find a way to get to him.

After all, those magnificent students of his were testaments to his worth as an educator.

"I'm here to save you, boss."

With her head held high, "Meadow" Sara came valiantly rushing into the train.

Here, the clock rewinds a bit.

Immediately after Klaus's disappearance was discovered, the CIM put their plan to assassinate White Spider into motion. Realizing that Amelie was planning on using the old train at the rail factory, they dispatched their finest agents to Queen Clette Station. The agents stormed the sleeping station and fired up its top-of-the-line locomotive.

Thanks to "Cursemaster" Nathan's leadership, they'd immediately pinpointed the train White Spider was on.

"A steam locomotive's performance is hugely affected by the talent of its crew. I can't imagine he's drawing out the train's full speed with some random makeshift stoker," Nathan calmly explained. "He can't

have gotten far. With one of our nation's newest steam locomotives on our side, we're certain to catch up with him."

Some twenty elite CIM agents had made it to the train in time for departure. And there was one more person standing triumphantly up on its roof—a girl who'd yet to remove her bandages.

"Heh. I was standing at alert should anything go amiss. 'Twould seem my prudence was warranted."

The girl had sharp features and dark red hair tied back behind her head. It was "Cloud Drift" Lan—the girl who'd been under CIM surveillance just like the Lamplight members. Her wounds were far from fully healed, but she'd begged the CIM to let her accompany them.

In her hand, she was clutching a bag full of weapons and the like.

"I'm code name Cloud Drift…no, perhaps another moniker would suit the occasion better."

As the steam locomotive began chugging along, she cried out with pride.

"I'm code name Insight—and 'tis time we soared the heavens."

However, not everyone on board that train was a friend to Lamplight.

The battle of intrigue had been defined by its countless traps, and now both sides were deploying their final aces in the hole.

Chapter 5

Bird of Fire

Twenty minutes before Sara rushed to Klaus's aid...

Just after she entrusted Klaus's rescue to her teammates and just before she used up the last of her strength, a spy came to see Sybilla. It was a man adorned with jangling ornaments whose hair went down to his waist. "Fascinating. I never imagined that Amelie would be the traitor."

Over to the side, Meredith stared at the man in shock. "Mr. Nathan?!"

Based on his reaction, Sybilla inferred that the man was a member of the CIM's senior leadership.

The man looked at Sybilla. "How elegant," he complimented her. "She laid a trap for both sides to get them to destroy each other, did she? That's well within Amelie's powers...but then, you cleared up the misunderstanding and reached an amicable resolution."

"Yeah, I guess so."

"Pandemonium, was it? I can see that Klaus is raising some fine pupils." His bangles jingled as he combed back his hair. "Rest assured I'll be offering whatever assistance I can. Serpent slew Prince Darryn, and I refuse to let them escape."

With that, he borrowed Meredith's radio and began giving orders to his agents across the city.

* * *

Determined to get Klaus back, Sara and Lily blitzed their way down Hurough's main thoroughfare on a motorcycle.

"Miss Lily, do you actually know how to drive this thing?!"

"Don't talk to me right now! I'm giving it my best guess!"

"Your best *what*?!"

After stealing the large motorbike they found in front of one of the nearby houses, they'd hot-wired it to force the engine to start. Lily was clutching the handlebars, and Sara was clinging tight to her back.

Right as they arrived at the building where Klaus was being held, they saw a suspicious car driving off. Upon spotting someone that looked like him in the back seat and realizing how panicked his Belias guards were, they decided to follow the car. However, they soon lost sight of the car itself in the night fog, and they drove through the city guided mostly by guesswork.

"I know where Amelie's goin', Lily!"

Eventually, Sybilla's voice crackled through their radio.

"The CIM figured it out. She might be tryin' to use the railway! Apparently, she got in touch with someone at a rail factory before this all started goin' down!"

"The railway?! How's a motorcycle supposed to catch up with a train?!"

"What's your current position?"

Sara read out the street name on one of the nearby traffic signs.

A few moments later, they got their reply. Sybilla had been consulting with the CIM agents. *"...You're not gonna make it."*

Her voice was pained.

At the moment, the CIM was mobilizing. Upon realizing that they couldn't get to the factory in time, they decided to gather up the spies near the station and get on the rails themselves. However, that plan was too slow if they wanted to save Klaus. White Spider could easily have already killed him by the time they caught up.

"Puppeteer" Amelie had arranged the board perfectly.

As horror washed over Sara, Lily spoke up. "Is there a route we can take to circle ahead of them?"

"Huh...?"

"Desperate times, desperate measures. What if we used the Seltin Bridge to board the train from above?!"

"What?!" Sara cried.

Lily slammed on the brakes to change their course.

"*...Copy that! I'll get you that route.*"

In addition to Sybilla, they could hear the flabbergasted CIM spies behind her. "*...Is that teammate of yours all right in the head?*" "*Ah-ha-ha, that's certainly an option we didn't consider!*" Lily ignored them, and once she had her directions, she took off in a straight line.

Eventually, they arrived at the bridge.

The Seltin Bridge was a grand piece of architecture that spanned a river on the city's outskirts. It had stood for over a century and been renovated several times in that span. The bridge had two levels: the roadway on its upper level, and the railway on the level beneath. All told, it was four hundred feet long.

When they arrived at the bridgehead, Lily brought their motorcycle to a stop. The train was nowhere to be seen yet. They'd successfully cut ahead of it. Now the only problem was how in the world they were supposed to get onto it as it barreled down the tracks.

"Aren't we just going to get run over?!" Sara very rightly asked. When the train got there, it was going to be moving at over sixty miles an hour.

"We're gonna go full pedal to the metal, then jump!" Lily shouted. "This is one of the emergency plans Grete thought up."

"What?"

"She thought up hundreds of different scenarios, all to protect Klaus. That girl's devoted to a fault."

The road running on the top section of the bridge and the train tracks running on its bottom were overlapping, but after clearing the river, the road continued on straight whereas the tracks veered to the right. That meant the train would have to slow down just before the bridge's end, and theoretically speaking, Grete believed it was possible to jump over.

Even confined to a hospital bed, she was still fighting, and she came up with a plan that had struck a group of CIM spies speechless.

"I'm not gonna let Grete's passion go to waste. This time, it's our turn to save the day." Lily squeezed the throttle. "As Lamplight's leader, I refuse to back down."

"........"

Inspired by Lily's dauntless courage, Sara began to work up her nerve as well. Klaus was going to die if they didn't do anything, and if White Spider got away, then they would lose any chance they had of saving Monika.

Right then, they heard a noise so deep it seemed liable to shake the bridge itself. A powerful orange light tore through the fog. The steam locomotive was coming. A minute from now, it would be entering the lower section of the Seltin bridge they were standing on.

"The train's here!"

"Then here we go!!"

As Lily revved the engine, a realization dawned on Sara.

Wait, we won't be able to see the train until we've already made the jump?!

Once the train entered the lower section of the bridge, Sara and Lily would have no way to visually track it from the roadway directly above. Landing on the train the moment it came out of the bridge would be all but impossible. The problem seemed so obvious in retrospect, but that was the issue with not having enough time to prepare.

However, the train wasn't going to wait around for them to figure it out. Within ten seconds, it was going to vanish from sight.

"Don't you worry." Lily gave her a soft smile. "You already know the solution. We've got Avian on our side, remember?"

The moment Sara heard that, she felt like a weight had been lifted off her shoulders. She took off her cap and squeezed her eyes shut in prayer.

In her mind's eye, she visualized the Avian members who were right there with them.

Avian's boss—"Flock" Vindo—stood atop one of the Seltin Bridge's arches. He was a man with brown hair, and his sharp gaze was fixed on the motorbike down below. As he watched Sara and Lily begin their attempt to jump onto the train blind, he let out an exasperated sigh. "I swear, you Lamplight girls take recklessness to a whole other level."

Vindo was an inspiration to the girls. He'd been promoted to being in charge of an entire spy team just a short while after he graduated from his academy. He was fiercely determined to surpass Klaus, and the girls had nothing but respect for his competitive drive.

"This'll be the last bit of backup I ever give you," he said, his voice forlorn.

Then he took off at a dash across the arch. Taking advantage of his jumping prowess and tremendous sense of balance, he charged down the bridge and hurled himself into the empty air.

"I'll be your landmark. Don't hesitate, just follow me," he declared. "It's time to take this Lamplight-Avian joint mission and bring it home."

Lily had the motorcycle on full throttle. The front wheel came dangerously close to lifting off the ground, but she narrowly managed to keep the bike going straight across the bridge despite its sudden acceleration. They'd built up enough speed now that when they jumped to the train, they weren't likely to get knocked off due to the speed difference.

However, that train had entered the lower section of the bridge and disappeared from view.

The end of the bridge was fast approaching.

Suddenly, Lily let out a shout. "I can see it!"

Sara looked up, and sure enough, she could see him. He was floating there in the night sky and marking their destination.

"I can see the path we need to take through the air!"

If Lily had hesitated for even a moment, it all would have ended in disaster. But if there was one thing she was good at, it was holding her nerve when the chips were down! She never so much as touched the brakes, and she veered at full speed over to the footpath beside the roadway and took advantage of the curb's height to send the bike flying in the air. They cleared the guardrail and went careening through the night sky.

"AHHHHHHHHHHHHHHH!"

Right as Lily and Sara got hurled into the air, they spotted the train running right below them. Seeing its massive frame race through the darkness stirred up a primal sort of terror in them.

The good news was, they were moving at practically the same speed it was, and the jump had been timed perfectly.

The next problem, then, was the landing. If they screwed that part up, they wouldn't live to regret it. However, the heat from the steam billowing out of the train's smokestack knocked Sara off-balance. Her body began spinning forward. Right as she braced herself for the worst, Lily gave her arm a firm yank.

The two of them landed on the train's roof, with Sara falling directly on top of Lily's left shoulder.

"———?!"

Lily let out a squeal of pain. They'd stuck the landing, but Lily's shoulder had taken a serious hit. She fell to one knee and clutched it with gritted teeth.

"Miss Lily?! You sacrificed yourself to—"

"GO!!" Lily shouted, urging Sara on as intently as she could. "Don't stop moving! Don't hesitate, just go!"

Sara sprang into motion, not even taking the time to nod in assent. She took the gun from Lily, dashed across the train's roof, and put her hat back on.

Lily was down for the foreseeable future. Even if she was in any state to fight, she wouldn't be of any use on the mission without a weapon or the use of her left shoulder.

The only one who could save Klaus now was Sara. She jumped down to the coupling and threw open the door.

Lamplight and Serpent had laid their schemes, and the battle was reaching its endgame.

When Sara rushed into the train car, she started by taking stock of the situation. The first thing she saw was the body lying on the floor.

Amelie...

Sara hadn't personally spent time with the woman, but she was still a spy with deep ties to Lamplight. It wasn't clear why she'd betrayed the CIM, but she must have had a good reason.

Sara also discovered that Klaus was still alive. He was kneeling on the ground by the carriage's back door, the one that Sara had just come in through.

"Boss..."

"Magnificent." Klaus nodded. "Thank you for coming to save me. It couldn't have been easy."

There was blood gushing from his right leg. The wound was fresh—he'd been shot. His hands were tied up, and his legs were both injured. He was clearly in grave peril, but Sara had gotten there in time.

That said, he wasn't going to be any help in a fight. Sara didn't have the means to free his arms. Those were special CIM-made restraints. It would be one thing if she had access to time and tools, but those were two luxuries she didn't have at the moment.

Sara stepped forward to shield Klaus as she turned her gaze to the man across from him.

"It's just you?"

The man's voice was cold and composed. Sara had never met him before, but she knew exactly who he was. He was the mastermind behind Avian's demise, Prince Darryn's assassination, Monika's entrapment, and all of the chaos engulfing the Fend Commonwealth and Din Republic. He was White Spider.

White Spider was bleeding from both arms, and there was a bruise on his face from some sort of blow. However, he was still standing tall, and he had the confidence on his face of a man who was more than ready to keep fighting.

He readied his gun and frowned in displeasure. "Nah, there's no way you could've jumped onto a moving train without getting at least a little banged up. So, what, you had two people take the jump, and your buddy's outta commission after breaking your fall? Can't think of any other reason they'd be hanging back."

After quickly analyzing the situation, he gave her a dismissive shrug. "So what'd you come here all on your lonesome for?"

"To defeat you."

She managed to get the words out loud and clear. She wasn't trembling or catastrophizing like she normally did. She was long past that point.

A lot of people put in a lot of work to get me here.

Sara could never have taken on White Spider alone. Grete, Sybilla, and Lily had all sacrificed themselves to make this showdown a reality, and they were all united in a common goal: to capture White Spider, to find out where Monika was, and to make it back to Din with all of Lamplight intact.

It didn't matter how powerful her opponent was. She needed to overcome him.

Sara held her gun in both hands and drew a bead on White Spider.

"All you've got for weapons is a single gun, huh?" When White Spider saw her get ready to do battle, his mouth curled into a smirk. "Shit, Amelie, you really are the gift that keeps on giving!"

The moment he tried to move, Sara pulled the trigger. The bullet soared straight at him…but then something blocked its path.

"——?!"

She hadn't seen him draw it, but there was a knife in White Spider's left hand. He must have blocked the bullet with its blade.

As Sara gawked in astonishment, White Spider swiftly closed in on her and fired off a front kick. She took the blow straight to the stomach and got sent crashing against the passenger car's rear wall.

"Sara!!" Klaus cried.

She promptly tried to get back to her feet, but a wave of nausea crashed over her and sent her reeling. The attack had hit her right in the solar plexus. Her sense of balance was shot, and she tripped over her own feet and collapsed.

All it had taken was a single hit, and she was already on the verge of unconsciousness.

Everything…hurts…!! I think I'm going to be sick…!

She planted her hands firmly on the ground and did everything she could not to crumple to her knees.

White Spider had blocked her bullet like it was nothing. Guns were supposed to be the ultimate form of weaponry, but he hadn't so much as flinched. As far as Sara knew, that was an advanced technique only shared by Guido, Klaus, and Monika.

This was a fight between spies who were on a whole different level than her. Sara had known that she was outmatched, and now she had cold, hard proof.

That gun was the only means of attacking she had. Amelie had confiscated all her other weapons. It was that, and her porcelain knife that was little better than a plaything.

But if I don't protect the boss here...

She fired off a suppressing shot, not even bothering to take aim. The bullet flew off in the wrong direction. All she'd accomplished was wasting her ammo.

"Look, I get no joy out of punching down." White Spider backed off and put some space between them. "Do us both a favor and jump off the train, wouldja? All I care about is killing the freak."

In no world was that going to happen.

After struggling back to her feet, Sara planted herself back between him and Klaus. With ragged breaths, she desperately forced oxygen back into her body. "I won't let you do that!"

"Oh, okay. Then you can die, too. Either way's fine with me."

White Spider took aim. There was a casualness to his movements, like he was simply removing an obstacle, but he wasn't getting sloppy. It was a logical conclusion based on an accurate reading of Sara's capabilities.

"........."

Sara had no ability to dodge or parry bullets. If things devolved into a shootout, her defeat would become a certainty.

She needed to find an angle, anything that might give her some tiny edge.

"We..." She put up the best brave front she could in an attempt to rattle White Spider. "We've got Avian with us."

"Huh?"

"Beating you will be a cinch! Haven't you heard? I think there were whispers going around the CIM about it," she blathered. "Avian is alive. Mr. Queneau gave Miss Annette a chunk of metal in her hospital room, and that's not the only thing they've done for us. I hear they saved Miss Sybilla just now. Miss Pharma helped her see through her opponent's lies, and Mr. Vics brought the ceiling down."

She gave him a triumphant grin.

"And they're still supporting us even now. The only one here backed into a corner is you. The whole reason we were able to make the jump onto the train is because Mr. Vindo guided—"

She trailed off midsentence. She'd just looked up to gauge her opponent's reaction, and when she saw the expression on White Spider's face, her breath caught in her throat.

The man looked bored out of his mind.

That wasn't the kind of expression you'd see on a spy in the middle of a mission. No, that was the expression of a person looking at someone they felt bad for. Someone they pitied.

White Spider awkwardly scratched his head. "Ugh," he sighed as he lowered his gun. All the motivation had drained from his voice. "Man, way to spoil the moment."

"Huh..."

"That was your big plan? Feels like I'm watching a baby crawl into the boxing ring as us dudes are trying to beat each other senseless. You didn't just kill the mood, you fucking buried it."

"What are you talking about?"

"Calling what you just said a bluff is an insult to the art of bluffing," White Spider snapped, making no effort to hide his annoyance.

Sara tried her best to riposte. "B-but they really are—"

"It was your animals, right? I've known you were an animal handler for ages."

White Spider took his hand off his head and pulled on his fingers to pop his knuckles. "I figured out you had a hawk, a pigeon, a dog, and some mice back when I was surveilling Lamplight. Then Amelie filled me in on some interesting news. Apparently, they found some hawk feathers in Forgetter's hospital room. You had your hawk do the delivery, right? That's who 'South Wind' Queneau really was."

"........"

"Now, the seeing-through-lies bit was what, the dog? You're not the first spy I've heard of teaching their dog to do that. That accounts for 'Feather' Pharma. Destroying the building, that'd be the mice. There are plenty of stories about mice causing big accidents chewing through gas lines or electrical wires. That's how you explain 'Lander' Vics."

He looked at his fingers as though he was just killing time now.

"And as for how you jumped onto the train—"

Without any warning, he nimbly brandished his gun and fired. Sara was so taken by surprise, she couldn't even react.

The bullet pierced her hat.

Gray feathers filled her view, and the chubby pigeon that had been hiding under her cap tumbled to the ground.

"Mr. Aiden?!"

"—you sent your pigeon on ahead and used him to set your aim. That was your 'Flock' Vindo."

Luckily, the bullet had merely grazed the pigeon's feathers. However, he was still in no condition to be moving around. Sara had been planning on using him as a diversion of last resort.

"Bottom line is this," White Spider said, sounding almost bored. "You've been shooting your mouths off about Avian this and Avian that these last few days—"

He paused for a moment, then went on.

"—but it was all just *fantasies*. Avian is dead and gone."

"——!"

Sara bit down hard on her lip. Everything White Spider had just said was true.

It was what Annette said—that "South Wind" Queneau had helped her—that gave Sara the idea for the plan. Annette had been making it all up. Either that, or she'd seen him in a delirious fever dream.

In truth, Sara had sent her pet hawk up to the hospital room out of concern for Annette. The window had been left open for ventilation purposes, and Sara had told her hawk to deliver Annette a piece of scrap metal without Miné noticing.

Then an idea had dawned on her—the off-the-wall plan of insisting that her pets were actually Avian. Her hope had been that it would confuse the CIM and give White Spider a scare, but apparently he'd seen right through her.

"We were there when Avian died, remember?" White Spider snapped at her. "I can't believe you thought you could get away with telling lies that flimsy."

In the end, Sara had failed to steal a win in the battle of deception, too. Her bullshitting skills just weren't strong enough.

But we still...

She desperately mustered energy in her legs.

We still have—

"You've got a look on your face that's saying 'We still have the Insight plan,'" White Spider said as though he could read her mind.

Sara froze.

Insight was well and truly the final card left in Sara's hand. If White Spider had come with a counter, then it would crush her last hopes of victory once and for all.

"When that Monika chick told you to deploy some mystery spy... Yeesh, that gave me a good scare. We were talking about someone I had zero data on." He scoffed. "But then you guys left me a hint."

"What...?"

"You lot were awfully close with Avian. You'd have to be, to go and revive their corpses like that."

Sara could feel her blood run cold.

White Spider's mouth curled into an ominous sneer. "All I'd heard was that Lamplight and Avian happened to run into each other on a mission once. But if you people were actually thick as thieves, then all of a sudden we were looking at a whole different story."

He stared at Sara to gauge her reaction.

"Code name Insight...is 'Cloud Drift' Lan, the one survivor from Avian."

".........!!"

Her body trembled. Shock rattled her brain, and her heart felt like it was about to stop.

White Spider nodded mockingly. "But hey, if I'm wrong, I'm wrong. End of the day, it doesn't matter who Insight is. I covered my bases and made sure there was *exactly one way to catch up with this train.*"

"You did what?"

"It should be, what, about three minutes before the CIM train catches up with us?"

He was right. The CIM weren't just sitting idly by. Upon realizing that Amelie had betrayed them, they raced to the station and commandeered a top-of-the-line steam locomotive. Insight was on board that train.

However, White Spider had accounted for that.

A foul grin spread across his face. "It's gonna be a massacre."

Over in the train car with the CIM's best and brightest, Lan was focusing with all her might. She took deep breaths to steady herself. Her wounds were far from healed, but she had an important job to do. What she was about to do would be the key to saving Lamplight.

Beside her, the CIM agents were anxious. All of them were in the same boat as her. Flash Fire had carved terror into all of their hearts, and the man they were going to capture was one of her fellow Serpent co-conspirators. Their senses of fear and duty weighed heavy on them.

As tension crackled through the carriage, something changed.

It happened right when they were passing through the Seltin Bridge.

"Who's the guy in the hood?"

The question came from one of the agents. He'd just spotted an uncannily tall man wearing a thick hood over his head in the next car over. The man was coming their way. His stride was bold, and the sound of metal scraping against metal was audible under his garb.

Eventually, the man entered the carriage that Lan and the agents were in. "White Spider never disappoints. Looks like everything's proceeding as planned."

Under his hood, they could see that the man was smiling. And extending from his long torso…there were three right arms.

"By intentionally leaving a way to save Bonfire, he gathered all the strong in one place."

The sudden appearance of a trespasser was enough for the CIM agents to draw their guns. Each and every one of them was a first-rate spy in their own right. A single intruder was nothing to be afraid of.

However, they'd chosen the wrong man to go up against.

"Now, the Unrivaled purge can begin—Surmounters, avail me."

* * *

The moment the agents opened fire on the man, he brandished his three right arms—or rather, the two of them that were glinting mechanically. Something akin to an explosion burst out of them, blasting all the incoming bullets off course.

Those prosthetics had just released a shock wave.

It wasn't clear how the process worked, but whatever the man just did, it created a wall of air that had blown up the seats directly in front of him.

Lan knew exactly who that man was. Vindo's dying message had described the people that killed four members of Avian. One of them was Green Butterfly, and the other was a man with many arms.

She rose to her feet and let out a roar. "YOUUUUUUUUUUUU UUUUUUU!"

The many-armed man stopped his tracks and turned to face her. "Ah, so it *was* Cloud Drift? Heh, good to finally know Insight's identity."

The amusement in his voice made Lan's blood boil. She recalled now that Monika had told them this man's code name. "Thou'rt Black Mantis, are thou not?"

"I truly am the Unrivaled. How far my name has traveled. Ah, goodness me. Perhaps this means I will never know peace." He sounded enraptured. "Once again, retirement inches away from me."

Lan wasn't the only one livid at how unserious he was being. The CIM agents opened fire again in an attempt to bring Black Mantis down. However, thoughtlessly poking the bear was the wrong move. This was the man who destroyed Avian.

"Wait! He's too—"

Lan tried to call them off, but they didn't listen.

"Get out of my way."

Black Mantis's prosthetics whirled into motion and began firing off more of those unidentified shock waves. Walls of air came crashing out, shooting the bullets out of the air and crushing the arm of the woman closest to him.

His weapon combined offense and defense into one, and there in the train car, there was nowhere to run.

Thus began Black Mantis's slaughter.

* * *

Bodies were rent and burned and blasted. The blades on the sides of the prosthetics tore through a heavyset man's torso like paper. The jets of flame gushing from the prosthetics roasted a group of spies brandishing guns. And with each shock wave he fired, bullets scattered and pulverized the arms and legs of anyone nearby.

No human should have been able to wield such power. Those two prosthetics had the destructive power of bona fide weapons of war.

Lan wasn't able to get anywhere near him.

The shards of wood from the seats Black Mantis destroyed rained down on everyone in the back of the passenger car like shotgun pellets. Lan's leg was grazed when she failed to evade successfully, and she was one of the lucky ones. The agent next to her got impaled in the chest and died instantly.

"AHHHHHHHHHHHHHHH!!"

Someone's scream echoed out, then immediately went silent.

The sound of the train's wheels was terribly loud. Black Mantis's prosthetics had done a serious number on the carriage's walls and roof. One of the corpses rolled out of the huge hole in the side of the car.

The massacre had been as swift as it had been one-sided. Lan hadn't been fighting, and she was the sole survivor.

Black Mantis stood motionless among the piles of bodies littering the carriage. "Hmm......... My Surmounters really are out of peak condition." He ran a disappointed hand across the prosthetics attached to his right arm. "What a shame. Were I fighting at full capacity, I would have been able to go kill Bonfire. But with their controls on the fritz, I ran the risk of destroying his restraints."

Apparently, this wasn't even his full power.

It made sense that the catastrophic destruction he'd caused wasn't intentional. With how damaged the carriage now was, his own safety was in jeopardy.

Black Mantis did a practice swing with his prosthetics, lashing out with them like a whip and obliterating a nearby corpse.

"Still, killing you will be child's play."

He knew that Lan was still alive. He slowly advanced toward her position.

Lan couldn't move.

That was the man who'd butchered her Avian teammates. She understood that, but there was nothing she could do. She couldn't envision any path toward victory. No matter what she tried, those prosthetics would simply kill her. However, there was nowhere for her to run in the train car, either.

If twenty elite spies had failed to defeat that monster, how was she supposed to beat him?

Once he got within ten feet of her, Black Mantis came to a stop.

All Lan could do was cradle her legs and cower in misery.

"No survivors. I refuse to let anyone go to Bonfire's aid."

There was still some distance between them, but she was well within his prosthetics' striking range.

He held his extra arms aloft.

"...............'Out of peak condition'?"

The words spilled from Lan's mouth.

Black Mantis froze.

For a moment, everything in the carriage was still. The only noise to be heard was the sound of the train's wheels chugging along.

"And why is that, prithee tell me?" Lan looked up. "Why is thy weapon broken, here at this eleventh hour?"

The question had nothing to do with the fight to the death they were in. It was just a question—nothing more, nothing less. However, Black Mantis froze like he'd been stabbed in the gut. Lan had hit him right where it hurt.

That said, it was a perfectly legitimate question. By all rights, shouldn't Black Mantis have been the one to kill Klaus? He himself had admitted that that was the original plan. Why had that changed?

"Did someone break it?"

Whoever it was, they must have been a truly outstanding spy. There was no reason for Black Mantis's weapon to be malfunctioning aside from outside interference. Someone had gone and wrecked his prosthetics.

"'Twasn't Dame Monika, no. As I hear, she was in no state to fight."

The answer was right there in front of her. It was intuition that led her to it, but more than that, it was faith. "Ah, I see," she murmured with joy as a tear rolled down her cheek.

"'Twas Brother Vindo and the rest who did the deed."

Lan had no proof of that, but it was the truth. She knew it.

"And so what if they did?" Black Mantis growled. His voice was a touch deeper than usual, and he was unable to fully hide his irritation.

"That should be obvious, should it not?!" Lan cried, spurred on by the delight welling up within her. "It means that you lost to Avian! Belias's surprise attack left them drained, and you had every advantage when you descended on them, yet they managed to damage thy tools of the trade! What is that, I ask you, if not a defeat?! Avian hath bested thee!"

Now Lan saw what had really happened. Vindo, Vics, Qulle, and Pharma hadn't just gotten mowed down. They'd held their own against an absolute powerhouse, and in doing so, they'd accomplished something great: wrenching Black Mantis, one of Serpent's members, off the front lines.

"Tell me I'm wrong! Were you at your strongest, you may well have succeeded in choking the life from Sir Klaus. Yet you were forced to change your plan. A shame, to be sure. And all because Avian destroyed thy appendages!"

"Are you done saying your piece?" Black Mantis raised his two prosthetic arms once more. "In the end, they still died. None of that changes the fact that you're about to join them. I'm a busy man. I have no time to waste listening to the whining of a sore loser."

"Which of us is the sore loser, I wonder?"

A cheeky smile flashed across Lan's face. Courage surged through her body. There she was, thinking she couldn't move, but now she felt as light as if she'd sprouted wings.

She still had no way of beating Black Mantis, of course, so she grabbed her bag.

"Rather than giving you the pleasure of killing me, I would sooner leap to my own demise."

* * *

She took off at a dash toward the hole he'd busted in the side of the train.

Black Mantis made no move to stop her. He realized that there was no need to launch an attack, and a moment later, Lan's body melted away into the darkness. The train was going at over sixty miles an hour. Even if she survived the fall, that wasn't something you could walk away from.

After checking to make sure that she'd actually jumped, Black Mantis turned around. "...It matters not. I carried out my duty."

Then he headed into the engine room and killed the engineers. Little by little, the train that been going to save Klaus slowed down, eventually coming to a stop in the mountains.

"Nobody's getting to you, White Spider."

After delivering his report to White Spider via radio, he hopped off the train and vanished into the darkness as well.

"All goners, he said."

White Spider lowered his radio.

"Black Mantis got the job done. The CIM spies all ate shit, and Cloud Drift ended up jumping off the train."

Sara shuddered upon hearing the news.

Black Mantis.

He too was a spy whose strength exceeded the bounds of logic or reason. So many people had just perished, and Lan had been involved in the attack. It would be no surprise if she was dead, too.

White Spider stowed the radio back in his pocket. "Looks like your bag of tricks is running empty. You got any more reinforcements lined up?"

"........."

There wasn't a single person who could save her.

White Spider had laid out plan after plan in order to kill Klaus. He'd predicted every contingency and prepared for all of them, and he had no compunctions about taking lives or resorting to foul play.

Sara went pale and shuddered at the man's sheer tenacity.

"That was kinda exciting, so y'know what, here's another little tidbit for you."

With that, he casually made his reveal.

"That Monika kid is dead."

"No.................."

Her breath caught in her throat.

For White Spider's part, though, he clearly didn't consider it a particularly important revelation. He was wearing a careless grin and massaging his neck. If anything, it was Sara's shock that surprised him. "Wait, hold up, you didn't seriously think she survived, did you?" he said with a bemused laugh.

Sara shook his words out of her head. She knew that if she didn't, she was going to accept them as fact, and her heart was going to shatter. "You're lying..."

"I'm really not. Go ahead, ask the monster." White Spider gestured with his gun. "He can tell, right? He knows in his gut if I'm lying or not."

"Boss..."

Sara turned pleadingly to Klaus, who was still on his knees behind her. Klaus possessed an incredibly powerful intuition, and it gave him the terrifying ability to instinctively sniff out most lies the moment they left their speaker's mouths.

"Please, say it's not true. I'm begging you...," she choked. "He's lying, right? There's no way Miss Monika is actually dead, right?"

The look on Klaus's face was uncharacteristically grim. He stared at White Spider like his memories of the distant past were overlapping the present.

"The man isn't lying."

When the words hit Sara's ears, all the light drained from her world. The sound of the train faded away, and everything she could see looked unrecognizably distorted, as though the world had lost its contours. Her senses grew dim. She couldn't even tell if she was still standing upright or not.

She could hear the sound of wind inside her body. It was coming from the hole that had just opened in her heart. That, she could make out with terrible clarity.

Her mouth moved. "Why?"

"Huh?"

"Why do you do these horrible things?!" The man standing across from her barely seemed human to her anymore. If someone had told her he was an alien from space, she would have believed them. His values were just too diametrically opposed to hers. "How… How can you just take people's lives like they mean nothing?"

"'Cause it's the only choice we've got, us losers." White Spider let out a scornful laugh. "Or, what, you wanna tell me it's virtuous for the weak to fight fair so they can get their asses handed to them? Fuck that. If you don't win, you lose everything. I can't afford to get hung up on the details."

"So that's it?! As long as you're fighting for a cause, it doesn't matter how many people you hurt?!"

"No, it doesn't. Necessary sacrifices, the lot of 'em."

His eyes were tinged with madness.

"As the underdog, anything I do is justified."

Sara refused to accept that. She refused to accept that Inferno, Avian, Prince Darryn, the CIM spies, and Monika and Lan's sacrifices had all been "necessary."

A heat burned through her, reviving her lost senses. She was feeling an urge she'd never felt before—the urge to kill. The very core of her being was telling her that that man needed to die.

"And hey, if you wanna tell me I'm wrong…"

Upon seeing Sara clench her fists, White Spider bent his left knee and shifted into a combat stance.

"…then come at me. Go on. Beat me and prove it."

"HRAHHHHHHHHHHHHHH!!"

With a roar, Sara lunged at White Spider. She knew she didn't stand a chance in a firefight. If she wanted to bring down someone who could swat away bullets, she was going to have to go for an all-or-nothing gambit and beat him with her bare hands.

Monika had given her close combat training for use in emergencies, and the hatred burning inside her was drawing her potential out to its fullest. She charged straight at her foe and tried to pound her right fist into his face.

"You're finally fighting like you mean it..."

White Spider stowed his gun in his pocket. He tucked his knife back in his sleeve as well and engaged Sara empty-handed.

"...but that's not how the world works. Putting your life on the line doesn't mean you'll win."

He hit her with his counter.

Sara poured everything she had into her punch, but White Spider's fist flew past hers and smashed her in the face. All the speed she'd put into her charge simply magnified the force of his blow, and she went careening backward. It felt as though her face had just shattered, and she started reeling.

Sara couldn't overpower him. Rage wasn't enough to make up the difference between them. She braced her legs with sheer willpower, determined to fight on, but that was when White Spider hit her with his follow-up.

"You get it, don't you? You get how brutal it is when the weak have to stand up to the strong!"

The moment she staggered from the heavy right punch to her cheek, White Spider hit her with a body blow from the left. Her body rose into the air, and her limbs went limp.

"You get how helpless it makes you feel to get run the fuck over like this!!"

He didn't let her fall to the ground. Now that she'd lost any ability to fight back, White Spider lifted his knee and slammed her with a front kick with his entire weight behind it. That first hit she'd taken was nothing compared to this.

"You *get* it."

His finisher of choice was a bullet.

Despite having taken the shot in the middle of a fistfight, White

Spider's aim was true. If Sara hadn't reflexively stuck out her right hand, the bullet would have torn straight through her heart. As it was, ripping through her hand shifted its trajectory enough that it grazed her neck instead.

The combination of the shot and the kick sent her careening backward, and she rolled over to where Klaus was and landed in a heap. She heard Klaus let out an agonized groan.

Sara used her porcelain knife to cut off a strip of her shirt. After quickly bandaging her hand to stop the bleeding, she rose back to her feet.

"I won't…stop moving…," she said, echoing Lily's instructions as she positioned herself in front of Klaus once more.

"You're still standing?" White Spider frowned at her in surprise. He must have assumed that that would be enough to keep her down. His cheek twitched a little. "You seriously haven't given up yet?!"

Sara was insulted that he'd just written her off like that. "I *don't* get it!!"

"What?"

"I'm saying, I don't understand the grievances of the weak!" Blood trickled down her right hand, and she squeezed it tight as she spoke. "Because I'm! Not! Weak!!"

No matter how badly he beat her body, her will would never break. If you were weak, then it was all right to make people suffer? It was fine to kill as many people as you wanted, regardless of who they were? That was nonsense, plain and simple.

She held her head high and poured out her heart. "So yeah, maybe I'm an academy washout! Maybe I'm the weakest member on Lamplight! And maybe I haven't grown at all as a spy—but still! I've been so blessed by every single person I've met." Every word she said, she meant. "You could search the whole world over, and you'd never find someone as fortunate as me."

Right when she was on the verge of flunking out of her spy academy, Klaus had found her, and Klaus had decided that she, meager as she was, was magnificent. Lily had cheered her on. Sybilla had laughed with her. Grete had guided her. Thea had supported her. Monika had taught her. And Erna and Annette had buoyed her spirit with their adoration. Then there were the Avian elites who gave her the tools to fight.

How could someone so blessed possibly be weak?

"That's why, right here, I can say with full confidence that I'm strong!"

She and White Spider were polar opposites. She was appalled that someone with his level of skill and strength could ever call himself weak.

"Who's coming to save you, then?" White Spider shouted in agitation. "If you're so blessed, then prove it. You're just a pathetic nobody, clinging to delusions!"

"They're not delusions." Sara raised her right hand high. "Avian never stopped saving us, not even here at the very end."

It was like she was trying to summon someone, and White Spider bit his lip in annoyance. In his defense, it was a natural reaction. There was no one who could rescue her from her predicament, and he knew it. No human being could possibly catch up with a running train.

However, Sara didn't budge, and she valiantly raised her hand all the same.

"How many times are you gonna make me say it?" White Spider snapped. "Everyone on Avian but Cloud Drift is dead. All those sightings were just your animals—"

"And we were counting on you figuring that out."

The moment the words left Sara's mouth, White Spider froze.

The shock Sara had felt when he announced that Insight was Lan came from the realization that their plan had succeeded. And the only reason she'd been shaken up when she learned that Lan might be dead was because that fact was sad in and of itself.

"That's what kept you from realizing who Insight *really* was."

A small smile spread across Sara's face.

It was time for Lamplight's final trump card, code name Insight, to join the fray.

◇◇◇

"Cloud Drift" Lan lay prone and gasping beneath the trees growing beside the tracks.

"E-every bone in my fingers doth ache…"

When she jumped off the train, she used her specialized Detainment string to grab hold of the trees next to the railroad and soften her landing. It was certainly better than hitting the ground full-on, but the damage to her body was still tremendous. Some of her fingers had practically gotten ripped off, and only time would tell how much long-term damage she'd taken.

"But I successfully kept thee hidden."

She opened up the bag she'd been holding between her legs.

"I take it we've drawn close enough for you to make it, Insight?"

The spy had been hiding inside the bag. He fixed his sharp gaze on Lan.

Tears of remorse spilled from Lan's eyes. "I beg of thee, make them pay."

She clung to him. She hated Serpent so much, but all she'd been able to do was flee. He was the only one she could count on.

She didn't know if her words had gotten through to him, but he continued staring straight at her.

"Thou'rt truly the symbol of Lamplight and Avian's bond. I can imagine no bird of fire more fitting than thee."

She couldn't move her fingers, but she gently rubbed them against his brow.

"Speech is no strength of thine, so allow me to speak in thy place once more."

Emotions surged up inside her, and she poured all of them into her words.

"Soar the heavens, Insight, O phoenix ours."

And with that, code name Insight *slowly spread his broad wings.*

After grabbing hold of the bag, he flew up into the air, caught the wind, and shot off.

They'd gotten close enough for him to catch up to his target. He couldn't sustain it for long, but his top speed was enough to overtake a train. And while the train had no choice but to follow the bends and curves of its track, he could pursue it in a single straight line.

He could feel a violent heat burning in his wings. He needed no words to know what his duty was. The time had come for him to carry out his mission and save Lamplight.

He'd been watching for so long, and that was what spurred him on. He'd been attending to the girl Sara and observing the team Lamplight for longer than anyone. He'd seen them grapple with their first mission. He'd seen the Lamplight girls' smiles. He'd seen how kind the Avian elites were in spite of their haughtiness, and he'd seen the tears Sara had shed in her quest to defeat White Spider.

Insight had been by the girls' side since the moment Lamplight was formed.

His wounded shoulder still ached from the time he'd taken that hit from the maid assassin's grenade. However, he refused to let it slow him down.

His thoughts turned to the partner he'd shared so much of his life with. Ever since she joined Lamplight, she'd started smiling so much more. He owed the team a great debt for that, and now it was on him to muster all of his strength repaying it.

The entire passenger car shook from a fierce vertical impact. The whole train very nearly derailed and toppled onto its side. White Spider's feet rose off the ground. It was all happening so fast that he couldn't react.

Then the window shattered, and the carriage's ceiling and part of its wall went up in flames as fire rushed in from outside.

What the...

White Spider's thoughts raced as he hurriedly fought to regain his balance.

Did they set off a bomb? Did they somehow sneak one on?

That was probably Flower Garden up on top of the locomotive. Had she thrown it, perhaps?

Nah, that doesn't work. They got stripped of their weapons, and they didn't have time to go grab more.

Besides, if Lamplight had access to weapons, then there was a far more efficient strategy they could have pursued. All they had to do was attack the people in the engine room, stop the train, and make a break for it. That would have been a far more promising option than having Sara fight White Spider all on her own.

In other words, their backup must have finally arrived, and that was who threw the bomb. It was the only logical conclusion, yet that too was impossible.

No human being *could possibly have gotten here!*

It was a normal premise to be working under, and it was one that he was unable to get past. White Spider had carefully sealed off any and all ways to catch up with the train.

And that was precisely the blind spot that Lamplight's plan revolved around.

Back before they set out for their mission in the Fend Commonwealth, Klaus had gathered the girls in the main hall and introduced them to a spy.

"I'm thinking of adding a new member to Lamplight."

As always, his explanation left a lot to be desired.

"This here is code name Insight. Here in the world of espionage where betrayal is a constant, you'd be hard-pressed to find anyone more loyal than him. He's the one spy I trust more than anyone else."

""""""""Okay, hooooooooooooold on a minute.""""""""

The eight girls all waved their hands in alarm. After their one unified rebuttal, the conversation turned hectic.

"Look, I get he's trustworthy, but still!" Sybilla said.

"Does he really count as a new recruit?" Thea mused.

"Lamplight's official roster consists of the eight of us and the boss, so...I suppose that would technically make him a new member," Grete replied.

"But is he really a spy?" Erna asked.

"I think he's a better spy than Sara, yo!" Annette chirped.

"Yeah, seconded," Monika agreed.

"Y-you know I have feelings, right?" Sara whined.

The girls' shock continued on for a good long while, but Lily eventually said, "W-well, I guess I'm happy to have him," and in the end, the girls greeted their new teammate with a round of applause.

At that point, Klaus resumed his explanation. They'd faced off against Serpent a number of times, and there was a decent chance that some of Lamplight's info had gotten leaked. They were going to need a new plan if they wanted to keep pulling the wool over their foes' eyes.

"There's a condition we need to meet before we can put Insight to work," Klaus stressed. "We need to convince our opponent that Insight is human."

Then, during the mission, that moment came.

It was Monika who primed the trigger. When she was facing off against White Spider and Black Mantis, she made sure that her voice reached her enemies as well.

"Get code name Insight. We need them. They're the only person *who can beat Serpent."*

The others immediately understood the implication behind her words. They needed to get their stories straight and convince their enemies that Insight was a person. But there was one girl in particular that Monika was truly betting on.

White Spider hadn't realized it yet. He'd yet to arrive at the notion that Insight might not be human. As soon as he realized that Avian was secretly just animals, he misjudged Sara's talent. In truth, though, the secret objective behind the "resurrect Avian" plan was to convince him that she'd used up all of her animal-related tricks.

It was a con that only Sara could have pulled off.

Avian had taught them a new way for spies to fight, a way to combine technique and falsehood into one. Sara had spent her life treating her animals with as much care and devotion as if they were human beings. That lifestyle had given rise to a unique form of deception, and she'd used it to create a fighting style that was all her own.

Rearing × Anthropomorphizing = Scrolls of Frolicking Animals.

The train rapidly decelerated. The driver must have slammed on the brakes. The passenger car jolted again from the force of the inertia.

As White Spider was losing his balance, Sara got moving.

"Code name Insight…"

She summoned all of her strength and shouted out his name.

"…MR. BERNAAAAAAAAAAAAAAAAAAAAARD!!"

White Spider had yet to successfully regain his footing when he saw it. Sara was dashing straight at him, and the moment she drew his attention, something came flying at him from his peripheral vision.

That something was a huge, dauntless hawk soaring through the flaming window. But as it flew through the flames, White Spider saw it as something else entirely, something straight out of legend.

A phoenix.

After appearing out of nowhere, the hawk hacked at him with its beak in an attempt to gouge out his throat.

"————————!!"

Too late, the truth dawned on White Spider. The hawk was Lamplight's secret plan. The hawk was Insight.

How the FUUUUUUCK was I supposed to figure that one out?!

The realization left him dumbfounded.

After smacking away the hawk snapping at his throat with an elbow strike, he turned back to face Sara. Sara was drawing a bead on White Spider using only her left hand and racing toward him to make sure she didn't miss. Her tag team offensive with the hawk was flawless.

She was too close for White Spider to defend himself with his knife now.

So this is what she was after, White Spider groaned to himself. Insight had never been a spy who could turn the situation around all on his own. However, the moment White Spider got the notion into his head that the spy had to be human, it created a psychological blind spot. Lamplight's whole plan had revolved around this single surprise attack.

Sara pulled the trigger. "You're finished!"

"Like hell I am, dumbass!"

In that final do-or-die moment, White Spider hurled one of his weapons of last resort, his miniature bombs. It went off so fast it wounded White Spider, but Sara got caught in the blast as well. Her bullet went wide and missed its mark.

A look of horror crossed her face. "……!!"

If there was one thing White Spider had going for him, it was the tenacity with which he cheated death. Sara had bet everything on that attack, and he'd endured that, too. She couldn't beat him. There was no overcoming the disparity in their skills.

"Looks like you've used up every last plan you got!" White Spider staggered as he raised his gun to shoot her dead. "And wouldja look at that! Now, it's time to bring an end to this once and for—"

"I gotta say, Master Bernard, you never fail to deliver."

That was when he heard the fearless voice coming from behind him.

Distracted from firing, he whirled around and found "Flower Garden" Lily standing right there. She'd been clinging to the top of the train the whole time. Her shirt's left sleeve was torn, and she'd wrapped a strip of it around her shoulder as emergency first aid.

She must have been the one who took the explosives from the hawk and set them off.

"Master Bernard brought me a lovely little present, see."

There was a sinister grin on her face and a rod-shaped weapon clutched in her right hand.

"Annette said she'd make a special weapon just for me, and now it's finally finished!!"

What even is that thing?

The weapon Lily was holding was like nothing White Spider had ever seen. As a matter of fact, it didn't even look like a weapon at all. It looked like a children's toy. The object was composed of a five-foot-long metal pole with a series of odd handicrafts on its end.

It was a pinwheel.

It all started with the promise Lily and Annette made back in the United States of Mouzaia's capital.

* * *

"When we get back to Din, you should build me the best weapon ever. Something strong enough to take down Teach."

"You got it, yo. With my tinkering and your poison, I'll be able to whip up something real nasty."

After her failed attempt at murder, Annette had devised a whole new method of killing. She realized now that she could get *other people to kill on her behalf* without ever needing to get her own hands dirty. In a sense, her evil had evolved and sent her down a path to becoming even more wicked than before.

The weapon had been imbued with the murderous instinct necessary to survive in a world as cruel as theirs, and Lily gave it a befitting name.

"This is Last Code: Paradise Lost—a spreading world of decay."

The pinwheel whirled, and massive amounts of foam frothed out from within, filling the inside of the passenger car with a speed and force that put all of Lily's past weapons to shame.

The bubbles were made of poison and inflated with poison gas, and with them, she'd seized complete and absolute control over the space.

The poison foam began engulfing White Spider. He tried shooting the bubbles, but they just kept on coming, and each shot he fired seared his nostrils with the poison gas that got released. What's more, the bubbles were covering Lily so completely that he couldn't even draw a bead on her.

I'm not going down, not like this!!

He knew there was no fighting back against something like that. He took a big step back in an attempt to escape the foam, but a figure stepped in to block his path.

It was Klaus.

Forcing his wounded left leg into motion, he charged in front of White Spider.

You monster...

White Spider was helpless to do anything but bite down hard on his lip.

"Goodbye, White Spider."

Klaus smashed his left foot into White Spider's face.

"...You aren't qualified to be my enemy."

After taking hits in succession from Sara, Bernard, Lily, and now Klaus, White Spider keeled over backward, and his body sank into the pinwheel's noxious foam.

Epilogue
Retirement and Legacy

"...and that concludes my mission report."

Back in the headquarters of the Din Republic's intelligence agency, the Foreign Intelligence Office, Klaus finished detailing the events of their long operation to the agency's spymaster, C. Klaus had been sending in progress reports as well, but he felt it was important that C hear everything that happened from start to finish from Klaus's own mouth.

He told C about how tracking down the truth behind Avian's deaths had led them into conflict with the CIM, he told him about how they'd gotten sidetracked upon discovering Glint's betrayal midway through the mission, and he told him about how they ultimately fought and defeated White Spider, the mastermind behind the whole thing.

"That's why it took so long for us to get back. My team was hurt pretty bad."

The mission had taken a harsh toll on them, and nary a single Lamplight member had emerged unscathed. In the end, they spent another full month in the Commonwealth just recuperating after beating White Spider.

During that time, Prince Darryn's funeral took place without incident, as though all that brutal spy fighting had never even happened. The procession carrying the body to Shalinder Abbey had been visible from Lamplight's hospital rooms.

"The good news is, we managed to retrieve Gerde's legacy," Klaus said with a nod. "All in all, it was a successful mission. It is a shame about Avian, of course."

Once he was done, he took a sip of the god-awful coffee C had brewed for him. The flavor made him wonder if he wouldn't have just been better off eating the beans raw.

From across the table, C gave him a round of applause. "Excellent work." It was rare for him to give out genuine compliments like that. "You never disappoint. You tracked down the cause of Avian's deaths, dealt with the cause, and even recovered Gerde's legacy. Three whole missions, and you completed them all."

"I suppose we did."

"But there's one part you left out, isn't there?" C's raptor-like eyes narrowed. "Is Glint dead?"

"........."

That was a point Klaus had specifically avoided touching on. However, that wasn't going to fly with C. Klaus was going to have to tell him. He was going to have to say those words he never wanted to.

"She's dead. We were too late."

His mind turned, and he thought back to the shocking conclusion they'd arrived at after defeating White Spider.

A gunshot rang out.

Right after Klaus forced his injured leg back into action and White Spider sank into the poison foam, the Serpent member offered one last show of resistance.

The bullet failed to hit Klaus, Lily, or Sara.

The poison foam and poison gas had left White Spider completely unable to move. They could see his body crumple to the ground below the bubbles.

Paradise Lost was a truly terrifying weapon. Born from Annette's twisted mind, it took poison gas and skin-searing poison foam and combined them into one. The former could be largely neutralized by holding one's breath, but the latter was a menace. Together, they gave Lily the power to seize control of an entire area.

"Fuck, man..."

Eventually, the bubbles faded away and revealed White Spider's collapsed body. He could still talk, but his limbs lay motionless. He'd used up the last of his strength.

"For a weakling, you really know how to make my life difficult." On seeing him, Klaus couldn't help but be impressed. "You took that tiny opening, and you used it to kill yourself."

"Shut up, man. This shit ain't me."

That final bullet White Spider had fired had been meant for himself. He'd been too off-balance to aim for his head, but he'd succeeded in shooting himself through the abdomen.

Blood gushed across the floor.

It wouldn't be long before his life ended. Klaus had wanted to capture him and pump him for info, but it looked like that option was off the table.

"Just tell me one thing." Sara helped him stay upright as he moved over to White Spider. "What happened to Monika? Did you really kill her?"

"The first thing you ask about is how your subordinate died, huh?" White Spider jeered, only able to move his mouth. "Quit making me repeat myself. I offed her. That's the honest truth."

Sure enough, he wasn't lying. Klaus's honed spy intuition told him that White Spider meant every word. "What did you do with the body?"

White Spider shut up. "........................."

Sensing the reason behind his sudden silence, Klaus's eyes went wide. "Don't tell me you—"

"I never found the body," White Spider sighed in resignation. "That moron Black Mantis brought the whole damn building down. Then he went and burned the rubble. All over a stupid little insult—but still, there's no way she could've survived that. Serves her right, if you ask me."

He hadn't actually witnessed the moment of her death.

Right as Klaus wondered if there were more hints he might extract from the man, White Spider spoke up. "Welp, looks like I'm outta time," he said. "Heaven's calling. Man, you really do boil my blood."

The life was fading from his voice. Klaus still had a million things he wanted to ask him, but if there was one thing White Spider was good at, it was running away.

"Rainbow Firefly."

A pair of words dribbled from White Spider's mouth—words that Klaus had never heard before.

"...What's that?"

"Hey, beats me. I don't even know why I said it. I just felt like I should say it to you, one pupil of Guido's to another."

"Who is it? Another Serpent member?"

"Wouldn't you like to know. Don't worry about it, man. It's just a prayer. Just a curse." White Spider's body grew weak, and the light drained from his eyes. "Fuuuuck..."

That expletive ended up being the last word he ever said. Through to the bitter end, he never stopped being a petty loser.

Klaus let out a long sigh.

He was dead tired. It had been a long while since the last time he'd braced himself to die.

I guess it's all finished... Our mission here in Fend is done.

That Black Mantis man had long since fled, no doubt. His job had been to assist White Spider, not assassinate Klaus, and now that White Spider had failed, Black Mantis was probably in the wind.

Had they really failed to save Monika?

He didn't want to admit it, but the cruel reality of the situation came crashing down on him all the same. It had been six days since she got attacked. The fact that they hadn't seen any signs of life in all that time meant that—

"...The basement."

Sara spoke the words softly.

"——?" Klaus turned his gaze over to her.

"Did you ever hear the story, boss? About where Gerde trained Mr. Vindo?"

"I got the broad strokes. Granny G dragged him to her hideout and—"

"R-right, exactly. I heard the same thing. I happened to be there when Mr. Vindo was telling Miss Monika about it..."

Her voice trembled as tears welled up in her eyes.

"...and Gerde's hideout has a basement."

* * *

They got to work immediately.

Not even Serpent would have had any way of getting the details about Gerde's hideout. If White Spider didn't know that run-down wooden apartment building had a basement, it would have been easy for him to misread the situation.

They gathered up every available Lamplight member and rushed to the village of Immiran as fast as they could.

On their way there, they met up with Lan. She'd fractured every bone in all ten of her fingers, but she followed along anyway, and Sybilla, Lily, and Sara all prioritized the search over getting treatment for their own injuries. Thea had just been freed, and she guided Annette, Erna, and Grete there from the hospital as well. In the end, every single member of Lamplight joined the operation.

When they got to the spot they suspected Gerde's hideout had been, they were greeted by a massive pile of weather-beaten debris. That was where Serpent had fought Monika and burned the building to the ground.

There was a chance that Monika had fled underground, and the debris had sealed off the basement behind her.

While they were searching, Sara spent the whole time apologizing. "I-I'm so sorry! If I'd just mentioned it earlier—"

"Don't you dare apologize! Even if you had, we wouldn't have been able to do shit with the CIM watching us anyway," Sybilla shouted back as she used her battered arms to heave aside rubble. "And besides, the CIM told us they'd searched the area! Who the hell woulda figured they missed somethin'?"

"They said there wasn't a body at the scene," Lily continued with a bandage wrapped around her left shoulder. "When they told us that, we all just assumed it had been removed!"

"B-but," Erna said as she diligently worked, "is she going to be okay? It's already been six days—"

"It rained for days on end after she was attacked," Thea said calmly, and Grete followed up on her comment as she helped carry away chunks of the wreckage. "That's right… The building above was destroyed, so it's entirely possible that rainwater flowed all the way down to the basement. As long as she had water, she might very well have survived!"

Meanwhile, Annette was using some hammer-like implement to smash through the burned wood. "I bet she kicked the bucket from the wounds that Black Mantis guy gave her, yo."

"His weapon was defective!" Lan called over as she scoured every inch of the ground. "Brother Vindo and the others smashed it. I daresay he was at less than his full strength."

Every person there was injured. The majority of the girls either ought to have been in the hospital or needed to head there posthaste.

However, not a single one of them stopped digging.

Eventually, Klaus found it. "Here."

There was an opening in the ground buried beneath the rubble. It led to a ladder, and after hurrying down it, they arrived in a spacious room. The liquor bottles scattered across the floor made it pretty clear they'd found Gerde's hideout.

They shined their flashlights around. The room was full of haphazardly strewn documents, their ink bleeding from the rainwater.

Eventually, their lights landed on the girl sitting in the corner.

"Is this a dream?"

Monika was *still alive*.

The sight stole the breath of everyone present.

The first person to rush over to Monika was Lily, who called out her emaciated teammate's name and wrapped her in an embrace.

"Y'know, if this is what the afterlife is like…then maybe dying isn't half-bad."

Despite everything, her expression was as snarky as ever, and she fell onto Lily.

Once he was done reminiscing, Klaus let out another exhale and continued giving his false report. "Everyone's better off with Glint dead anyhow. The majority of the CIM still views her as the culprit behind the crown prince's assassination. The Republic can't afford for her to still be alive."

He said it all in a single breath so as to demonstrate just how stern of a spy he was.

"On a completely unrelated note," he continued, mustering up the most cheerful voice he could as he changed the subject, "I was thinking of accepting a new member onto Lamplight."

"………………………………………………………………"

C was silent for a long, long time.

Then he frowned at Klaus in suspicion. "If she was alive, you should've just come out and said it."

"I'm sure I have no idea what you're talking about, but she betrayed the Din Republic. Even if she had somehow survived, I have no idea what kind of punishments you would have in store for her."

That was why Klaus hadn't wanted to bring up the topic. He would hate for it to look like he was harboring a traitor. Glint was dead…as far as the paperwork was concerned.

"Code name Ashes—that's the new member I want to add to the team."

She was like a raging fire, melting that glinting ice and revolutionizing the world by burning everything to ash. The name "Glint" didn't suit her. Not anymore.

When Klaus left the Foreign Intelligence Office headquarters, he found the girls all standing outside. The first thing he did after returning to Din was go straight to headquarters rather than stopping by Lamplight's base, but at no point had he asked the girls to wait for him. Many of them had yet to fully recover, and surely they wanted to get some rest.

"We promised we'd all go back together," was Lily's argument.

They boarded the train and began making their way back to the port city they were based out of.

As an aside, there was a major fracas between Monika and Annette during their journey back to Din, but that was a story for another day. Annette's grudge ran deep, but they eventually managed to settle things amicably.

The group went through the secret passage together, and when Heat Haze Palace came into view, Lily let out a bellow. "WE MADE IIIIIIIIIIIIIIIT!"

""""""""WHOOOOOOOOOOOOO!!""""""""

They threw their hands in the air and let loose the yells rising up in their chests. Their cheers of joy were fervent and nearly deranged, and they all exchanged teary hugs.

The mission had been grueling. Any of them could have easily died, and they'd all survived by hair's breadths. But all of them had made it back in one piece, and that was cause for celebration.

At that point, Klaus noticed the one girl who wasn't participating in the revelry.

"Our painting is gone."

It was Lan. She had nowhere to go, and she'd followed them all the way there.

She was staring at the outer wall of the manor. The rain had washed away the phoenix mural that had once adorned it, and almost nothing of the mural was left.

"'Tis but I that remain…"

She ran her hand softly down the wall. Right as Klaus was about to call out to her, though, she shook her head. "No, worry not for me."

Her voice was free of hesitation.

"Worry not for me, you all."

Klaus quietly stepped away. He felt it would be best to give her some time to herself.

When Klaus sat down to rest in the chair in his room, he heard the sound of knocking.

"U-um, Boss…?"

Sara opened the door and peeked in with her head hung as per usual.

They hadn't even been back for three hours yet. Klaus had heard cheerful voices coming from across the manor just a moment ago, so Sara must have intentionally slipped away from the group.

She walked over to him and gulped a little. "I know it isn't the best time for this, but do you have a minute? I want to get this out there before I lose my nerve."

"What's going on?"

"I want to retire from being a spy."

Klaus was taken totally off guard. However, her voice was confident. This wasn't some spur-of-the-moment decision.

"This last mission showed me something. It made me realize just how deadly this line of work is."

"...Well, that's a shame."

It stung to lose a valuable team member, but if that was what she wanted, he had no choice but to accept it.

As conflicted emotions stirred within him, Sara frantically waved her hands. "O-oh, no, that's not what I mean—I'm not saying I want to quit *right now*!"

"You're not?"

"I'm still going to work to support the team. But, um...I'm really just not as attached to this line of work as everyone else." She smiled. "So someday, when I reach a good stopping point, I'd like to retire."

Her face was brimming with forward-facing determination.

Klaus couldn't bring himself to be upset. He turned toward her. "Do you have an idea of what you're going to do afterward?"

"I—I do, yeah. I want to run a restaurant like my parents did. One in a quiet town, with a view of the sea, and with food that's really tasty but not too expensive."

"I can see you've put some thought into this."

"Lately, I've been thinking about it every day. Miss Annette and Miss Erna could be my waitresses, and I could cook, and all the others could work there, too." She hung her head in embarrassment. "A-and if that happened...then I'd really like it if you were there, too, Boss."

Klaus was struck speechless. He hadn't seen that one coming at all.

"I—I know it's all just a fantasy, of course," Sara stammered as a sort of excuse.

Klaus, on the other hand, had never ever considered fantasizing about a future like that. Could there be a life for him outside of espionage? It wasn't impossible. As long as he didn't die, it was certainly a way things could pan out.

"If that future came to pass…"

He gave her his honest opinion.

"…it might actually make for a happy ending."

It went without saying that Klaus had no intention of retiring. He'd inherited Inferno's duty, and it was his job to keep the Republic safe.

At the same time, though, he didn't want to reject Sara's vision.

"Then I'll keep working hard so that everyone can retire without reservations." Sara squeezed her fists in delight. "And until then, I'm not going to let anyone on Lamplight die—that's my goal as a spy."

Curiously, Klaus felt himself rooting for her.

Sara had never had a strong motivation for wanting to work as a spy. She'd been doing her best, but only because she had nowhere else to go and didn't want to cause problems for the others.

Now, though, she'd found an ideal and stated it clearly—becoming Lamplight's guardian.

She cared less about the results of their mission than about her teammates' well-being. Her priority was protecting the team, making sure everyone made it through their operations alive until they could all retire.

That was a perfectly respectable way to approach the craft, too.

"Magnificent," he said, praising her in his usual manner. "In that case, I recommend you focus on studying spy skills that you can use after you retire. I'm sure that understanding psychology and honing your forecasting skills will be invaluable in the world of business."

"I look forward to continuing to learn from you, Boss."

From there, one thing led to another, and Klaus ended up giving her a cooking lesson. The fridge was completely empty, so step one was going out to buy ingredients.

On their way to the entrance, they caught a glance of what was going on in the main hall. The girls appeared to be gathered around the table. They had a wireless transceiver, and they were all staring at it with a strange intensity.

The scene piqued Klaus's interest. "What are you all up to?" he asked.

The group gathered around the transceiver consisted of Thea, Sybilla, Grete, Annette, Erna, and Lan.

"Shh!" Thea said, putting a finger to her lips. "We're eavesdropping."

"On what?"

"We left Monika and Lily alone together."

"I can see how that would be fascinating."

Now that she mentioned it, Klaus remembered that there was a piece of unfinished business. Not even Monika herself had expected to survive that mission, and midway through it, she'd given Lily a message.

"I'm in love with you."

The rest of the team had all heard her loud and clear over the radio, making Monika's confession of love an extremely public one.

I would be lying if I said I wasn't curious about how Lily responds, but still…

It was so very like the girls not to even hesitate before planting a wiretap.

Thea was beside herself with excitement. "Heh, heh, heh. Don't you worry about a thing, Monika. As your partner in crime, and as the local love guru, I'll make absolutely sure your love comes to fruition," she muttered to herself.

She certainly meant well, but Klaus doubted her efforts were appreciated.

By the sound of things, Monika and Lily were out in the courtyard. Lily had gone out to check on the state of her garden, Thea had planted a wiretap on her, and Monika had just found Lily and was none the wiser to the bug's presence.

"Hey, Lily… I wanted to talk."

They could hear how nervous Monika was. It looked like they were actually going to get to hear the conversation, but—

"You can't!" Sara cried as she leaped at the transceiver.

""""""""Huh?""""""""

Sara snatched up the transceiver and clutched it between her arms as she turned it off.

"Let's just not! Th-this isn't right! Think of Miss Monika!"

"What do you think you're doing, Sara?!" Thea shouted. "It was just getting to the good part!"

The others cried out in agreement, but Sara held firm. "Nuh-uh! I'll protect you, Miss Monikaaaaaaaaa!"

She fled across the main hall still holding the receiver in her arms. The other girls chased her down, and the whole thing devolved into a violent game of tug-of-war. Their bodies may not have fully healed, but at least they were in good spirits.

I suppose rubbernecking is a bit classless.

Klaus decided not to take part in the scuffle. If he had to say, though, he tended to agree with Sara.

Through the main hall's window, he could see the girls' heads out in the courtyard. Lily and Monika were staring at each other with serious looks on their faces.

I can't imagine their conversation going anything but smoothly.

He had no idea what decision Lily would ultimately come to, but knowing her, he was certain she would find a thoughtful way to express it that took Monika's feelings into account to the best of her ability. And no matter what she said, he was certain that Monika would earnestly accept it.

They'd fought their way through a brutal mission to reach that moment, and they deserved to be able to have it to themselves.

After all, the world at large had no intention of releasing Lamplight from its clutches.

They found Gerde's legacy down in the basement with Monika. That was where Gerde had once trained Vindo. The room up on the third floor was a decoy. Gerde's true hideout lay beneath the ground.

There were invaluable documents strewn all about. *Classic Granny G,* Klaus mused, *not taking better care of her files.* The rain had flowed into the basement and blurred the papers' ink, but Lamplight still managed to decipher a few passages.

Within the next two to three years, there'll be a financial crisis—one so bad they'll call it the Great Depression.

Apparently, it was going to start in the United States of Mouzaia. Mouzaia had enjoyed an economic boom in the wake of the war, and they'd been overinvesting ever since. When that bubble popped, it was going to devastate every industry under the sun, and the ripples from that were going to be felt across all the nations that had grown dependent on the United States' economy.

It was unclear what point that "two to three years" number was counting from.

The nations of the world will prioritize their own economies and begin hoarding resources. Countries with colonies and strong economic foundations will prosper, and the Axis powers that lost their colonies in the war will suffer.

Many nations regretted the Great War and sought international harmony, but this will force them to quickly shift their policies.

A number of powerful figures, Prince Darryn among them, have sensed the tides shifting and are putting a plan into action.

When they read the next line, they froze.

It all made sense. That was what brought Inferno down. This was what gave rise to Serpent.

The hell that had brought the world and the girls of Lamplight so much pain was rearing its ugly head again.

A second world war will break out—and the Nostalgia Project is how they plan to prepare for it.

Secret Epilogue

Serpent

Code name Silver Cicada. Icedew Park, Bumal Kingdom. KIA.

Code name Blue Fly. Endy Laboratory, Galgad Empire. KIA.

Code name White Spider. Hyrin Railroad, Fend Commonwealth. KIA.

Code name Green Butterfly.

Escaped the CIM prison thanks to instructions from "Puppeteer" Amelie. Headed to a safehouse to arm herself but was ambushed by "Cursemaster" Nathan. Died from a blow to the chest. She, along with her old identity, Magician, were erased.

Afterward, Nathan declined to share this information with the CIM, his official organization, and instead conveyed it solely with another organization altogether.

Code name Purple Ant.

Escaped during a torture session conducted by the United States' JJJ intelligence agency when his interrogator took his eyes off Purple Ant for the briefest of moments. The phrase "Rainbow Firefly" was found written on the scene in blood. Purple Ant's legs were broken from the torture, so he'd been in no state to escape on his own.

Two months later, Purple Ant was found dead with a thin smile on his face.

◇◇◇

Code name Black Mantis.

Instead of boarding the smuggler's ship as planned in the south Hurough port, Black Mantis simply stared out at the night-darkened sea. The meeting time had come and gone, and Green Butterfly and White Spider were nowhere to be seen.

He sat atop the abandoned shipping container, sighed, and turned his gaze to the Hurough skyline off in the distance. His two prosthetics quivered as he mumbled to no one. "What a fool of a man. With this, you've left me no choice but to avenge *you*."

Then he sensed someone behind him.

Thinking that perhaps one of his comrades had finally arrived, he turned around.

"Ya-ya-ya, what do we have here? Looks like I found the Serpent survivor."

It was a young man. One he didn't recognize.

The youth was wearing a beige trench coat that went down to his knees and a pair of round glasses. His black hair was done up in a disheveled perm, and his features were muted, like a traveler from some distant land.

His footsteps echoed out as he walked with his hands deep in his pockets.

"Yeesh, I wish you hadn't killed my double. That was a real drag."

Black Mantis readied his prosthetics. "I have no memory of those I've slain. Name yourself."

"I'm Ouka." The youth gave him a faint smile. "One of the people your guy Purple Ant killed."

"………!"

The name was well-known in the intelligence community.

Purple Ant had murdered scores of agents during his indiscriminate spy killings in Mitario. The ranks of the dead had included Hearth and a number of other world-class operatives, and one of them had stood out most of all: code name Ouka, a mysterious spy who operated behind the scenes in countries across the world like a gentleman thief.

The youth had referred to a "double." Perhaps the code name didn't belong to an individual, but rather a group.

With another "Ya," Ouka drew his hand out of his pocket holding a gun.

"———"

Black Mantis blocked the quick-draw shot with a mechanical arm. However, that was no ordinary bullet. The smell of chemicals rose up into the air.

"I wouldn't use that arm anymore if I were you," the youth said.

Black Mantis had gotten doused in flammable liquid. If he wasn't careful, he might blow himself up.

"So you came to kill me." Black Mantis gave a small nod. "What's your aim? Tell me. We at Serpent are short on personnel, and we have justice on our side. If you beg nicely, I'm prepared to offer a spot at the bottom of the hierarchy."

"Thanks, but no thanks. I've already got my own place in the world," the youth replied. "With Cherubim, the grave keepers of the holy tree."

"Huh?"

"We're a team founded by Hearth, the Finest Spy in the World—and our aim is to see the Nostalgia Project to completion."

Black Mantis nodded. It made sense. Even in death, Hearth had a plan. By that point, she'd already made her move. Spies from across the world had been gathering in Mitario, and she'd taken advantage of that to build up a new force separate from Inferno.

So that was the choice her schism with "Torchlight" Guido had led her to…

"You're being awfully forthcoming with that information," Black Mantis noted.

"Personal policy of mine. I'd hate for someone to die without knowing the score, you know?"

"You're a funny man." Black Mantis rolled his shoulders. "I'm afraid I'm in the dark, so you'll have to explain something to me. How is it you intend to defeat me, the Unrivaled, and end my career as a spy?"

He held his prosthetics aloft and gazed up at the sky.
"Ah, I can feel retirement inching away from me."

Code names Indigo Grasshopper and ——.

Over in the Galgad capital Darton, there was an individual reading a book. They'd gotten it from their subordinate, Indigo Grasshopper. "Thought you mind find this interesting," Indigo Grasshopper had told them.

The book had been written by Fend novelist Diego Kruger and published posthumously shortly after Kruger succumbed to his drug addiction. It was a ludicrous spy novel that had been panned by critics as the worst publication of the century.

A single read was all it took for them to realize who'd truly penned it.

"Christhardt."

That was real name of the man they themselves had dubbed White Spider, the man who'd gathered up combatants and built Serpent up to make a stand against the forces of the world. He had been the heart and soul of the team.

The novel was packed full of fabrications, but as the story progressed, it became more and more clear just how much the protagonist loved his organization. For all his cussing and complaining, he did everything he could to bring them success.

Now, though, Christhardt was gone, and they'd lost contact with all the combatants he'd assembled.

"Who would have imagined that making enemies of the world would be such a trying ordeal?"

Serpent had failed. The spies Hearth left behind had overpowered them.

Was there really no way left for them to stop the Nostalgia Project?

"*Indigo Grasshopper,*" they said, calling to their agent by name. "*I want to negotiate with Lamplight. Would you be so kind as to send them a letter for me?*"

Before anyone knew it, a full year had passed since White Spider's death.

Afterword

The following contains spoilers for the main story. Please finish the book before reading.

I know the Volume 8 afterword isn't the greatest place for it, but I hope you don't mind if I take a moment to talk about my writing process for Volume 1.

I touched on it a bit in the Volume 1 afterword, but I wrote *Spy Classroom* by taking my winning entry to the 32nd Fantasia Taisho awards and completely rewriting over 95 percent of it.

That then begs the question, what was the sub-5 percent left over from the Fantasia Taisho era? I'll tell you: it's the idea of having one of the characters be a poison user, the fight on the boat, and Sara. I changed her name, but the character who was the model for "Meadow" Sara existed all the way back in the original manuscript. Personally speaking, I've known her for a longer time than I have Klaus or Lily.

That was why, back when I was writing the first volume, I decided that she would be the focus character for Volume 8. I knew she wouldn't get much of the spotlight before then, so I made up for that by ensuring she would truly get a chance to shine at the end. I try to show all my characters the same amount of love, but the way I ended up showing Sara hers turned out a little funky.

While I'm on the subject, there's another conversation from when I was writing Volume 1 that bears mentioning.

My original editor, O: "I'd love it if you could give each of the girls their own unique weapon."

Takemachi: "I totally get that, but the first book is already chaotic enough as it is."

After that discussion, I ended up putting it off all the way to the end of Volume 8. It finally showed up, Tomari! You gave it such a cool design back on the Volume 1 cover, so I felt terrible about not finding room for it in the books until now. Annette refused to build it, you see, and it took a ten whole books (including side story collections) to convince her…

Now, between the anime adaptation from Studio feel. and the concurrently running manga adaptations of Volumes 2 and 3, there's a lot going on in the world of *Spy Classroom*, but as far as the novels go, we're actually heading into the back half of the series now. I'm currently locking in my vision through to the final book, and I hope you'll join me on the rest of the journey. I daresay our male lead might even get a focus book of his own at some point.

Before we get to Volume 9, though, I hope you don't mind if I squeeze in Short Story Collection 3. The backlog of Dragon Magazine shorts is piling up, and this way, I'll be able to share tidbits from the Avian honeymoon in a way I didn't have room for in the main novels.

When we do get to Volume 9, though, it could very well herald a big change for Lamplight.

I'll do my best to make sure it lives up to your expectations. Until then, that's all from me.

Takemachi